INTO THE SUN

Charles Ferdinand Ramuz

INTO THE SUN

translated from the French
by Olivia Baes and Emma Ramadan

 A NEW DIRECTIONS PAPERBOOK ORIGINAL

Translation copyright © 2025 by Olivia Baes and Emma Ramadan

All rights reserved. Except for brief passages quoted in a newspaper, magazine, radio, television, or website review, no part of this book may be reproduced in any form or by any means, electronic or mechanical, including photocopying and recording, or by any information storage and retrieval system, or be used to train generative artificial intelligence (AI) technologies or develop machine-learning language models, without permission in writing from the Publisher.

Originally published in 1922 in French as *Présence de la mort*

Manufactured in the United States of America
First published as New Directions Paperbook 1642 in 2025

Library of Congress Cataloging-in-Publication Data
Names: Ramuz, C. F. (Charles Ferdinand), 1878–1947 author |
Baes, Olivia translator | Ramadan, Emma translator
Title: Into the sun / Charles Ferdinand Ramuz ;
translated from the French by Olivia Baes and Emma Ramadan.
Other titles: Présence de la mort. English
Description: New York : New Directions Publishing Corporation, 2025. |
"A New Directions paperback original".
Identifiers: LCCN 2025017190 | ISBN 9780811238663 paperback |
ISBN 9780811239639 ebook
Subjects: LCGFT: Science fiction | Novels
Classification: LCC PQ2635.A35 P713 2025 | DDC 843/.912—dc23/eng/20250410
LC record available at https://lccn.loc.gov/2025017190

10 9 8 7 6 5 4 3 2 1

New Directions Books are published for James Laughlin
by New Directions Publishing Corporation
80 Eighth Avenue, New York 10011

INTO THE SUN

*In memory
Of a summer when we thought
It could have been this*

I

And so the great silent words came; transmitted from one continent to the other over the ocean, the crucial message came.

Over the water, the crucial news traveled that entire night in the form of questions and answers.

Though in fact nothing was heard.

The crucial invisible words, of interest to all men, traveled and intermingled; however not one man, beneath at sea, beneath on land, heard these words—and nothing in the sky changed when these words came, and they were still coming.

The great words passed unseen,—unsettling nothing in the air above the merchant ships and the white transatlantic liners,—in a sky only noticed because its stars were larger than they had ever been,—and onward, over the offshore swell, the words passed in complete silence.

On that night, these words, then some questions and the answer to these questions;—and then for all men everything will change so much that they will no longer recognize themselves, but for the moment nothing changes; everything stays so calm, so incredibly calm on these waters, with dawn rising and against its beautiful white color puffs the smoke from a large ship no one sees.

Today as always, and as if this would last forever,—except that the great invisible words have been pronounced, communicating the results of lengthy calculations and meticulous research: the Earth is plunging into the sun.

Because of an accident within the gravitational system, the Earth is rapidly plunging into the sun, pelting toward it, to melt there.

And so all life will come to an end. The heat will rise. It will be excruciating for all living things. The heat will rise and rapidly everything will die. And yet for the moment nothing is visible.

Nothing is heard for the moment; everywhere silence and more silence. The message itself has gone quiet. What had to be said was said, and then, silence.

Morning arrived upon the sea where the ship was heading toward the horizon, that great slope made of other smaller slopes, which the ship tackles one after another, like an ant attacking one furrow after another.

II

The only sign up to that day had been the extreme drought. It was the end of July; the drought had lasted three months. A few stormy rains in June, a few fat coins still fell on certain nights that month, unexpectedly, on the pavement in front of my house: that was all. The hay had been beautiful, the harvest abundant and dense. It was after that the soil had begun to crack, the grass to turn yellow and sparse.

In sum, tracing these beginnings, there had been no unusual signs until the end of July. On the surface, nothing yet except this drought and this great heat, the thermometer having started to climb to 77 degrees in the middle of the day, then to 81°, 100°. And we did suffer a bit, but it was bearable, because the sky was so beautiful, and because we live by the lake. The lake is where we go to observe; the lake is where we see what's coming, which is to say that we see nothing, other than this beautiful vault never before so lavishly painted, as when a painter adds two or three layers, but because the good workman can never be satisfied, he says: "That's not enough."

We lived under the beauty of this sky. The high hollyhocks had dried above the yellowed parsley and the Chinese carnations, which had not even been able to open: this sky replaced everything. We said: "Yes, it's true, it's hot, but how beautiful!" And then: "We had hay, we had wheat!" We said: "It'll only affect the vegetables, but we'll find a way to live without them … And the wine will be excellent!" Our Lavaux winegrowers will have been happy on their last year, because of the promises made to them, although the vineyards had frozen in the highlands, as they say; but what was left would be good, would be extra good, as they also say, and if this continues, wishing only for a few warm and gentle rains, toward the end of August, so that the grapes would swell. And with a click of the tongue: "Not much, but extra good! And if the prices stay up …" And once more we would turn to the sky.

Because, you see, is it clean, is it varnished, is it scrubbed enough? could the color be any deeper? Above the little red roof of the shed and the round elder tree, all around the jagged holly, above the slope descending to and from the lake, above the water and the mountain. Above me and above us. Above us all. And enduring, this sky seems enduring, oh! so enduring! We thought: "It's eternal …" And so we must rejoice and find patience, because the fatigue will pass, and we are not very hungry and if we lose a little weight, we'll have the time to gain it back in the fall.

Alright! The gardener himself says: "Alright!" Guignet, the gardener, agrees with the people on this point, even though he's annoyed, because for him there is the watering issue, having planted his water umbrella right in the lettuce bed, but "it's dry two feet down and the topsoil is so hot that the water steadily evaporates," he says, pushing back his straw hat, spitting, grabbing his clay pipe from his pocket, filling it, and looking around at the vegetable garden.

There are flowerpots all the way to the edges of the paths for the mole crickets.

There is also a sparrow trap. Guignet puts the birds in his pocket for his cat.

This morning, we chatted again for a moment; no, not one sign, it's all so very beautiful!

Well, nothing but this drought, which we were confronted with once more when Guignet turned on the Bret water faucet; the pressure, it's true, has been dying down in the pipes: and so the water umbrella was no more, what remained was a half umbrella, what remained was a small circle of fine white dust around the pole.

It's getting a little lower every day; none left! It's getting lower; "So," said Guignet (having finally lit his pipe and blown into its stem, because it doesn't pull properly), "so what if we can't water anymore!..."

All the same, I continue to watch this oh so beautiful sky, shades of the lilacs' leaves hanging within it, all inside out.

Our Savoie, so gentle and beautiful, has come forward harshly; for several weeks now, we glimpse the mountain from very close up, as when bad weather would come; there is no longer any bad weather.

A few nights ago, around two in the morning, the shutters began to flap, the windows slammed shut, the doors were shaken, the roof tiles came tumbling. A great warm wind entered through the windows, which were kept open day and night. A great warm wind, blowing in from the south, from the mountains just opposite, fell upon us with its entire weight. I went to look. There was no trace of clouds. Only those very big stars, so white they made the sky look completely black. Stars like paper lanterns. Although this wind was so relentless it forced us to retreat, it made us even hotter. And we started to feel fear, but we weren't able to get to the bottom of this fear, because the wind had already stopped. Abruptly, and so completely stopped, that we immediately started to hear once more the ticktock of the watch on the night table;—

and once more, those same people go swimming, only now the great beach, as far as the eye can see, is dark with nude bodies.

In a little shop, a woman sells pastries. An ice-filled wooden bucket reveals the necks of some beer bottles. The people who have never gone swimming in their entire lives have come. On the keel of an old boat, a little old man sat, his cape over his knees, reading a book. His skin was so white that he looked tossed in flour. Nearby the giant boatman's body was the color of burnt brick, in other words a mixture of brown, red, and black. The little girls play "Rondin picotin"; the women are in swimsuits. Always this same great beauty of the sky, reaching above the poplars, those great black columns. The sand flows through your toes like water; there is sea glass of various colors, pretty round stones, flat or in the shape of an egg. Not one sign, except that it is all so beautiful. All these people, how many of them? The city completely empties each afternoon, and we watch people descend in every possible way,—by foot, by tram, by funicular, by bicycle, toward coolness, toward wellness; moving down toward another more agreeable temperature,—just like today, two big prostitutes sitting sensibly, their flowered hats on their heads, up to their necks in the water.

Some children, who arrived swimming, clambered onto the rudders of the passing steamers.

We see those same steamers, crowded with the people who like to go against the wind, beneath the flapping awnings.

Those same great white machines, with their wheels turning and smoke unspooling from their chimneys like horsehair coming uncoiled at the quilter's.

III

That's when the news arrived, first received in disbelief by the newspaper editors;—then suddenly, hoisted and emblazoned on the front page, like black and white flags, flags the color of grief.

The impact here, however, in those first days, in the beginning, was not very big. We don't have much imagination here.

There is the town that sprawls up there over its three hills; it allows the hourly strokes of the clock to keep rolling toward us, more or less of them, more or less spaced out;—that's about it.

This suburb is still quite rural, despite all the new construction. The evening paper arrives only around six o'clock and it's the women who read it first, while the men are still at work. A bit more time can pass here, amidst the continuing cries of children swimming, as the great sun descends as low as possible to meet the mountain. It's 88° in the shade tonight; nevertheless, no threat of thunderstorms, none of those large clouds there once were, white, sheeplike, or smooth and slate gray, or black; nor that heavy air there once was. The light, far from whitening, became more golden above those voices hailing from below. The blue of the sky became even bluer, if that's possible. All is well. In the café, there is drinking; in the grocery store, sugar is weighed, and in the boulangerie, bread (as always). And perhaps a great rumble already buzzes about the rest of the world: here there is only the sound of the streetcar, arriving at a snail's pace, and stopping in front of the café. Because it's empty, the employees go in for a drink. At that moment, a woman leaned out of the window, asking: "Have you read it yet?"

The voice of a woman from the floor below: "No."

On the third floor, the woman who asked the question adjusts her poorly buttoned white blouse; she is holding the paper. She reads the news aloud. The woman below then tilts her head back, reeling in a little girl whose hair she is brushing before bedtime, without stopping the quick movement of her fingers among the blonde strands.

And the woman above, having read, points at the headlines; but the other: "What do I care?"

This is the small start of nothing here, with no observable signs. The inventor of the idea is largely alone in his idea. The incoming news is received only with distraction or smiles. A night like every other night arrives on our roofs, fairly close together. It is the hour when the swimmers come back up, after having once more beaten the water with their two hands and tucked their sliver of Marseille soap into their striped trunks. Their shoulders are cooking beneath their shirts; the women have scarlet necks, the red of their arms is barely muted by muslin sleeves. Some mothers are late, pushing the little baby carriage where their youngest child sleeps and with the others following as best they can. Quick, because it's time to eat, and the husband will soon be home. Perhaps he's already home. Quick, quick, beneath the sun that is now red, red-orange first, then red-red, then red-black.

There is a farm on the way. In the farm's stable yard, we see the evening work underway. There are two or three men, including the owner; they come and go. They are focused on themselves. They imagine nothing beyond what they are. They consider a certain fixedness of things as being so fixed that it could never change. They move through time as if time will exist forever.

The wheelbarrow's only wheel turns in the same way as it did yesterday, and in the same way it will turn tomorrow. The wheel of the wheelbarrow cries. The cow closest to the door is visible from the road. There are red shutters. The barn door is red. There is an old fir tree bowing to the corner of the shed.

And yet, here too, the newspaper has arrived. A small, thin woman, her body crooked in her gray coutil bodice, is carrying a wicker basket in her arm, without knowing what's in the basket. She carries the newspaper folded four times, next to more of the same papers folded four times. She delivers it door to door. On the old bench painted green, which is against the barn wall, the owner, having finished his work, begins to read: but no, he hasn't understood. It's too big, that's the thing. It's not for us, it's too big. Our own world is so small. Our own world goes as far as our eyes can reach; it's our eyes that create it for us. The owner, perhaps looking around with a little worry in the beginning, has finished reading; the worry vanishes.

We would have to imagine the sky, the stars, the continents, the oceans, the equator, the two poles. Yet we can only imagine the self and what we have. This self and what we have are here. The proof: I touch, I reach my hand, and I touch. The owner sets the paper down on the bench, pulls out his pocket watch, looks at the time. He feels his hunger come to the surface.

IV

And then in the grocery store. Seven o'clock. Seven thirty.

"Ah! my God, my God, my God!..."

Just like that;—two, three, four, five times in a row.

A woman entered, and that's what she said, once, twice, three, four, five times, and nothing more; and then the grocer: "Madame Corthésy!"

All those barefoot children (and the boys are only wearing pants) are so shocked as they stare at her, holding their coins between two fingers, surrounding the large copper scale, polished and shining in the dimming light.

"What is it, Madame Corthésy!"

The good grocer with her big belly and on each cheek her small bouquet of red veins.

But, as her hands rise before her, the woman shakes her head, and her hands fall back down once more: "Well," she says, "just imagine, it could be true!"

Then, starting up again: "My God, my God!" Just imagine, imagine, imagine!

"What nonsense!" the carpenter then interjects. "The news comes from America, you know what that means. The newspapers weren't selling anymore, so what do you expect?!"

He continues to explain it, the local carpenter, a tall and thin man who seems shrewd,—standing before a piece of cardboard,

12

where the buttons of detachable collars have been sewn; continues on and on:

"They're not ashamed of lying ..."

So calm, his hands in the pockets of his green serge apron, smiling now and then, and then it begins.

"What do you want, Henri? ... and you, Georges? ... A kilo of salt; do you have a bag? ... Go and quickly fetch one from your mother ..."

Shop, telephone ringing, window display, jars, flies.

New customers, this time a man and a woman, two or three children; they go about their business, and the shopkeeper, while giving change for two francs, touches a finger to her forehead, because the first woman, Madame Corthésy, has just left.

A crazy, deranged woman. The shopkeeper does not dare to speak aloud everything she is thinking, because of the others, but the carpenter has understood. The shopkeeper and the carpenter exchange a look.

The carpenter sticks around. People come, people go, people come.

Bare feet make no sound on the sidewalk and none on the floor either, with all these little round freshly shaven heads closing in on one another.

Coins tendered, parcels picked up, bread, or a carton of sugar, or five cents' worth of juice; and on it goes, and the only sign is that those who come in take out their handkerchiefs and wipe their foreheads several times, because it would be useless to hope for any cool air this evening.

And a voice again:

"So, what do you think about it all?"

And the carpenter, still there:

"Not a thing."

He's laughing. He starts laughing again; but the other:
"Well! Who knows?"

And the other, who is a short and stout man, paunchy, popping in to buy a pack of tobacco, this man is half serious, but the carpenter has started up again: "Lies! Nonsense!"—holding his yellow pack with the green wrapper in his left hand without opening it, perhaps because he's trying to imagine what it would be like, and his pipe remains empty at the corner of his mouth, he doesn't think to fill it up.

He tries to imagine; it's too hard; he gives up.

He tears open the wrapper of his tobacco, he plunges two fat fingers into the opening.

Then, a shrug, a "Got to go!" and a "goodnight."

Sound of the scale.

The electric light shaped like a big moon, hanging very high above the road, turns on. With a crank handle, it is lowered from time to time to be cleaned or repaired. From above, it crackles as if a moth were caught inside its globe, then disseminates a fine purple dust. It looks like the real moon when bad weather is coming. And so we search for the real moon, and after a moment we've found it, over there, behind the rooftops, behind the chestnut trees, still so low in the sky and not any smaller than the other moon, but pale, so pale and immobile, as if painted as decoration in the sky with a brush.

The apartment lights are also turning on. On the facades of the houses, not far from the ground, there are white and yellow rectangles. The houses are no longer visible. Nothing but an indication of where we are and where we stand; something to tell you there are presences here, for the most part halfway up between the earth and a roof, elevated, overlapping rooftops; and we see how the people sleep on top of each other, how they nest like

14

birds. A pause in the noise; the children are being put to bed, it's dinnertime. What are they thinking about? It's almost time for them to take up their thinking once more.

There will no longer be just them, but now also the images of themselves that they create; no longer just the outside things, but also the things within the self. Suddenly, just like that,—when it begins here, it will expand, concentrically, around each little center, each heart, each love, each self-awareness;—but there's been no sign of it starting yet. The things that are created (if they are created) are things that cannot be seen. Silence. Far off, in the night, the streetcars are on the move; the last incoming steamboat has whistled.

And no lake, tonight;—for a long time now, no lake in the evening, nor at night; whereas before, always, the lake was there and it came; it came to you with its waves, each wave like a long phrase spoken quickly and quietly. Back when every two or three days a violent wind rose from the south: then the big voice came.

But no lake, tonight, and there has not been a lake for a long time; this perhaps is what is frightening, this perhaps is what has started to frighten us, this absence. Some sort of void, some sort of interruption. Those who pass on the road can feel it. And so everyone hushes, and hushes further, and on their own account. And there was the café also. After the grocery store had closed, the café grew and grew, its door with the flowered cretonne curtain and its green trellis pergola with its wisteria trunk made of many little trunks twisted together. Nine o'clock; and now the café's full. This is when a fist comes down on one of the tables. Not at the big one in the middle, but at one of the little tables on either side.

A man, who had already been sitting there for some time, shows the spot on the newspaper page to the two men who are with him; he trails one finger under the title; he says: "See?" to one of them, then to the other: "See?"

Then, he raised a hand:

"Pretty strange, huh? Because we are used to dying at our own time …"

He speaks louder and louder:

"Every man for himself, in his bed … They say that's all going to change … All together! … You … you … me … and them …"

He points to the people around him; and then, to each of the two men at his table, to one: "Come here!" to the other: "Come here!"

Laying an arm over their shoulders, then:

"I guess now I'll have to go and invite those gentlemen, too …"

He laughs.

"Because we'll hang onto each other's necks … We'll form a chain …"

But he was stopped:

"Shut up!"

It was one of the people at the middle table, because there was a great silence; and this man:

"I told you to shut up!"

With a mean voice, like someone who is frightened.

V

So quickly slide these eyes again across those waters, which, far from coming to an end, seem boundless as we rush against them. Once again, while I still can, and today, I allow for the coming and going of this smooth and vast surface belonging to me. Thirsting for you, one more time, O beautiful waters, to go against you and feel you coming and going, scanning you from top to bottom. These things that will be left behind, perhaps: and so to love them even more today, to know them even better. And to finally know this place, which comes and comes, greeting it, generous, varied, long and wide, abundant, truly vast,—in its solitude and its purity. With no landmarks on its surface, only the movement of our eyes indicates we are coming and going. All this water, which belongs to me, to scan it first with my eye, then, raising my eye little by little, to unravel it, until I crash into the stones on the other shore, until I raise the two small stakes, worn by the rope, of a landing dock, of the platform, and further the little square houses with their flat-tiled roofs, without gutters, whose foundations plunge into a new beginning of themselves, into their image upside down.

Here, in the middle of the land, is the mirror of the lake, where we see coming from the depths what must come, then there is the other shore and the opposite bank. We rise against it, it's elevated. Again, our eye moves up and down, caressing it. Once more, right? O things of over there, you too, dear bank and dearest bank: and we return there, counting them, lining up those ascending patches of planted meadows with their high and dry branches like polished bones, along which vines grow; their little patches of wheat; the layout of houses with the ruins of houses on the edge of the road, some on the first tier, some on the second; or a small chapel for the Virgin Mary, and behind its gate, a granite cross.

To go against this, to rise against this, having crossed the water with our eyes; to this, against this (once more)—and to tell you, list for you, count for you, the things of over there, dear things that are in front of me, and to bring myself to you once more, across the water, with my heart, as if on a boat, first greeting you from the open water, and then the open water disappears, the distance no longer exists; we come, we are here, we rise, we touch, and the already translucent grapes hang much higher than the hand.

A harvest which may not come, which is exactly why ...

The Savoyard had breakfast. The Savoyard carried the manure in his sack the entire morning, down the flat little path which occasionally passes over a stream, now very close to running dry, and with hardly a trickle of water left in the fountains. The madwoman in the street comes and goes. The Savoyard carried the manure in his sack, taking very small steps, then filled his pipe with contraband tobacco, tobacco from here, big black tobacco which has also crossed the lake, but in secret, and now the Savoyard blows his smoke toward the chestnut branches. Then he went home. The Savoyard had lunch. He heard the church tower's midday bell ring again, and, when the wind is favorable (the north wind is the favorable wind), the steeples of the other shore can also be heard ringing at midday. But not today. No one heard them today, those bells over there, they have not been heard for a while, for some weeks now the north wind has not blown, nor any other wind. What is happening? The Savoyard does not ask himself. Having carried his manure, the Savoyard has gone to eat lunch, and he eats in the kitchen, whose open doorway is filled by two different blues. A boat sits against the granite doorstep with its raised sail; this is the first blue. He, however, is sitting before his hollow yellow bowl where he dips his round tin spoon, which he only lifts a little, because he goes to meet it with his mouth. Sprawled out and settled, secured by the sturdy and secure table, he feels at home. As if he could last forever, with those things around him, which he does not pay attention to, because they are forever things, forever the same, which he does not see, which he has never even looked at;—and there is this double blue in the door and once there was a difference between them: now there is no longer any difference. The water has become like the sky in its shine and stillness, the difference is no longer visible; the Savoyard does not pay attention, the Savoyard sees only that it is there and has always been there. He lowers his mouth, he slightly raises his spoon; he has let his elbows spread wide, his shoulders are squared, his hat on his head;—on a big chain in the courtyard, the small dog barked, it's a passerby;—the Savoyard goes to sit a moment against a wall outside; the pigs are grunting, because the hour has come to feed them. Once more, his pipe is packed. And if we looked, we would see that the boat that was at the bottom of the doorway has now slightly moved, though there is still no wind blowing, but out on the open water there are currents that will do this;—so those on the boat, having eaten, they too, go lie down on the deck in the shade of the sails, that deceptive shade, that shifty shade, that unfaithful shade, an untrue shade, a shade that mocks you and lies ...

O Savoie! once more, and toward those over there, and toward those higher up, and also toward those who are at the edge of the water on the left, where their harbor is;—and, from behind the harbor's walls, the only things visible are all those masts sticking up, like a little dried-up forest that has lost all its leaves and its branches, yet still showing a little color, because those masts were painted, some white, green, red; but it's only from above that we discover the black hulls packed so tightly together that the decks seem to be one deck, one great floor for us all to dance on.

Oh! and this again, Savoie. To go again toward this, over there, and make it rise,—with the great boulders they blow up, gutting the mountain a little more each day, they pierce holes with the drill bit and fill them with cheddite; they take off running: on the road there are signs stopping the automobiles from passing, saying: "Stop right there!" to the passersby, waving to them from afar, stopping the baker on his bicycle.

The avalanche descends, the great blocks tumble down like a flock of sheep.

As the avalanche descends, the bang comes; the bang came toward us.

The detonation slowly came toward us, halting to hover above the lake, sometimes even forgetting to cross it entirely, stopping midway, renouncing any further moves;—and the other times, when the detonation came, it was long after, sluggishly bursting for us in the air, as when a big bubble rises to the surface of a pond…

VI

A man named Jules Gavillet, a broker, had worked in his office until seven o'clock, then had gone for dinner.

He found himself alone, on that night, because the friend he usually ate with was on vacation.

He had glanced at the newspaper; he had (like so many others) shrugged it off.

"We have calf's head tonight, Monsieur Gavillet," the waitress had said; he had responded: "That's fine."

He didn't have much of an appetite. No one had much of an appetite in those days, not long before the end. And Gavillet, having tucked the corner of his napkin inside his detachable collar, ate distractedly, all the while thinking about his business.

Through the window, always the same great stone-arched bridge, the same rooftops, the same passersby. The same streetcars, the same cathedral spire in the same spot in the sky. And Gavillet kept computing numbers in his head, while his jaw kept moving beneath his eyes, which seemed occupied, but it was only his inner calculator;—he was a man like that, which is to say like so many others, multiplying, adding, subtracting ...

They brought him the stew ...

Under the stacked numbers, a line is drawn with a ruler.

Care, all of our care is invested in this,—drawing a line in the sky above the bridge, the passersby, the rooftops, higher than the cathedral spire, which he continued to look at without seeing ...

21

Around 2,200, if everything went well.

2,200, 2,300,—"Anyway, let's see tomorrow, I've had enough for one day ...,"

And then, he saw that he was alone. There was a little wine left in the decanter, he poured it into his glass, he emptied it in one go. He saw himself alone in front of the little marble table and, simultaneously, through the window, the evening was closing in on him like a curtain. Terribly alone, all of a sudden. He had paid, he had lit a cigar. He was smoking his cigar, blowing out a plume with a round movement of the lips, the smoke a blend of gray and blue. What will I do with myself, what will I do until tomorrow? Question. There was a response to his question. It was a cinema, whose frosted sign has just lit up. You had to walk through the square; you had to walk down a street. A change was in the air; it was not so visible yet, but a change had finally come. Newsagents were still shouting the headlines, despite the late hour; there were groups forming on the sidewalks. Gavillet bought a second-class ticket. The show started with the Pathé News. The minister assists a regional costume parade in Brittany. That's Gavillet. Nothing, just an office worker. Just the beginning of a man, just a head for stacking numbers above and below each other. You could glimpse New York from atop the scaffolding of a skyscraper under construction, then the machine operator himself lying flat on a metal beam with his coffee grinder. O seas, rivers, shores, perspectives! those cars like flat insects, the men smaller and pointier. Spaces, turmoil, various directions, the harbor, the canals, the large avenues. The trains are like caterpillars, the big warships like pumpkin seeds ... There is the world, now it's gone. A light went out. Another came back on. The cinema was almost empty. But already, once more, the world, which had been hushed for a moment, began its chatter, the world which is great, which is a great beautiful thing, which comes to you, yearning to be loved. Which is filled with self-respect, which is proud of its power, which says: "You did not know me." Which is beautiful, which is sweet, which is sour, bitter, cruel, great, which is ugly. Which is deserted, which is filled with men, emptied of men, which is populated, which produces nothing, which produces everything. With cities, without cities. And the world: "Here I am!" and again: "Here I am! Get to know me." The world: "Look at me. I come at you, I thrust myself to you, I am everything." It comes at our faces, and we move our faces back … And now, it was the glaciers of the North Pole, their crevasses filled with black water, upon which a boat was carrying some men armed with rifles: and we see the bear, shot down with a bullet, get up on its hind legs, join its front paws over its chest like a lady with her hands in a muff, and then spin around several times …

How does the idea enter us? Gavillet watches, lets himself go; in the beginning he did not understand, after a moment he understands … It's over …

The light comes back on. Gavillet wipes his brow. The great heat is returning, driving away the imaginary cold. There are several realities. Gavillet looks absently at the posters on the walls, the padded seats, the Louis XV decoration, and the bright ceiling bulbs. Some poor people were sitting in third-class seats, the father, the mother, and two little girls. There were also a few workers with their caps on. A little farther, an old bald man reading his paper. A great silence had arrived; everything is bathed in the great silence and dull air where a few poor bodies remain: this is no longer reality. It's a false reality. And we were awaiting the former; all at once, it returned … A tumble of horses through sand dunes; on the horses, men in pointed hats shooting their guns …

Mexico. The southern United States, the borders with Mexico.

Guerrillas. Wooden villages. Armored trains. Shady cabarets where a dancer spins, while the door is swung open by a shoulder. Boxing matches ...

And there is love.

This love, with a lanky, flat figure and light eyes, whisks off the missionary's wife. He sits her down before him on his saddle. The image disappears.

He sat her down before him, with her modest high-collared bodice. A rocky desert where they gallop. The image disappears.

A gorge, an overhanging path they follow. The image disappears.

He lays her down on the bed, he looks at her ... O world, world, how far? how far are all these things of the world? how far into the hearts of men, these possibilities of the world,—such as love, desire, anger, all kinds of hate, all kinds of love and hate. There is a love that pretends and a love that resigns. There are contradictory loves. There are contradictions even in love ...

And it kept coming; and Gavillet, still there, received it all and sat clueless. The immensity of mankind was shouted at him from the depths of the unknown, as were all the beauties of the world, at this man who had never known anything, who was not, who was not yet ...

He had walked out; they were shouting the headlines of a Paris newspaper which had arrived on the night train; he bought one, unfolding it beneath the light of a streetlamp.

Telegrams were printed in bold headlines on one side of the paper. He shrugged, he crumpled up the paper and threw it away. He set off again. His white vest walked before him beneath a faint, dark-colored jacket, and as he walked between the trees of the dimly lit allée, his vest was the only thing visible. Here and there were electric orbs, each in a cloud of moths and mosquitoes.

There were palm trees planted in barrels. The lake, at some point, became visible between the facades of two villas, the moon's reflection on it like spilled milk. He took his master key from his pocket; he went up the stairs, up to the third floor. He walked on tiptoe, obeying his old disciplined habits. His room was at the end of the hall; he rented it furnished from an old maid. He flipped the switch. He saw the bed, he saw the air of great cleanliness reigning there, mingling with boredom, with something petty, lifeless, too methodical,—with the same bedtimes, the same mornings, the same nights, the same movement of bodies. As on every other night, he had draped his jacket over the back of a chair, as on every other night, he had folded his pants, wound up his watch, turned off the light. He had lain down on the bed.

He had turned off the light, he had crafted the night all around him: a light went on. The other light.

The world now living inside of us, which can't be stopped; the world which entered us without our knowledge and which we can't bar from entering.

As when a door in the house, which has always remained shut, is opened: the fresh air, and then the sun enters, and in May, the smell of beetles; and the mosquitoes that enter and the flies hoping to enter.

And we allow it all to enter, and it enters, and all is well, and then, suddenly ...

Because he had thought: "What if it's true!...."

It came back to him at that exact moment. He had just remembered the telegrams he had read in the paper. And, suddenly, there was life, but there was death also, which he had not yet known, because he had not known life.

Because one does not come without the other. One comes, the other comes also. One had not come, which is why the other had not either. Life had an intimate sister. You didn't marry the one or the other, you married both.

He had sat up in his bed.

In his imagination, he pushed out of himself the largest spaces possible, constructing each of them, but by the same process destroying them ...

He had never thought about it, he had not yet understood: you had everything, you had nothing; you had nothing because you had everything.

And, in vain, he tried to put it out of his mind, slumping backwards, folding his arm under his head like a child before sleep.

He was not able to sleep. He sat up, he lay back down. He got up, he turned on the light; he turned off the light. He sits, his head in his hands ...

He is completely astonished, at some point, to see light between his fingers, as the great song of birds begins to sound.

VII

This morning I will sit tight at my table, while I still can. My unpolished walnut table, with fluted legs and no drawers, not very big; unfinished wood, fluted legs, slightly higher than wide, nearly square; I will pull myself up to it, and, once I am right up against it, as if right up against reality, I will look.

I look also, I look at what is; I place here only what is. What can be seen through the open window of this ground-floor bedroom between its iron bars; and there is only the corner of a meadow with a tall wall to the right dressed in ivy; in the back, an elder tree which shakes like a small sea when there's a wind, a shed with a tiled roof; on the left, three tall poplars.

Nothing else before me at the moment, still only this garden corner, and we describe only what is there.

We describe only what is there, when the copper kettle has been placed on the stove and begins to sing. The porcelain filter is waiting, the coffee (once more) has been ground, once more grabbed in handfuls from its metal box, poured into the grinder between the knees, whose crank has been turned. And then came the sound of the drip, a very audible sound, because each sounds alone, as when a small pendulum swings ...

Sitting tight at my table: I place here only what can be seen.

What can be seen, this morning, is that, as always, the lake is nearly entirely hidden by the flat hillside, and the mountain too is nearly entirely hidden by the trees. I place here only what can be seen; what can be seen is that it's beautiful, that it's tranquil and beautiful. At first only the drip of the filter can be heard; next the cry of a bird, then the cry of no bird; now it is the voice of a woman, on a balcony.

I dip my quill into the ink again. I will live a little longer. I will look for as long as I can. Things, I am watching you, I can see you. Two, three, four, I am trying to count you. Where does your number end? how many are you? who are you? why are you? Then came the eight o'clock bell, and, once more, the coachman Besson hitched his horse in front of the shed, cursing, many words, and the sound of the pail he was dragging across the sidewalk. Like every other morning, his deep voice, his clogs coming and going. His deep voice, his clogs with their wooden soles; and then time, time is flowing ...

Besson's head peeks out from behind the raspberry bushes. It rose in profile beneath the straw hat, it rose on three occasions, in jolts, because of the three steps; it turned to face me. It came toward me. The horse in front. Besson in his seat. The cream-fringed parasol swings between the cedars and poplars. There are still plums on one of the plum trees; Besson's whip goes to fetch one.

It falls onto the parasol. Time is flowing. Write down only what can be seen. Slowly, allow things to happen. Each thing going, in front of us, at its own little speed; as the branches rise and descend, during each second, the flower opens a little more and without our realizing it, the leaf moves, the leaf spins around the stem in both directions, back and forth; and the drip of the filter continues, and time continues.

There was, once more, the drip beating the measure of time, like some sort of small pendulum, but which had already exhausted itself, having drained itself little by little of everything it contained ...

A tram passes behind the solid wood door of the courtyard, painted gray. I boarded the tram. I go to the front platform, where a sign reads: *No Speaking to the Conductor*. Beneath that sign, the conductor. The glass windows have been opened wide, so that the air can circulate. Two or three men stand near me; one of them says:

"Ten years earlier, ten years later ..."

He shrugs.

Another asks him:

"How old are you?"

"Fifty-three."

Silence. We keep going. And it is only after a while that someone starts up again:

"Ten years, that's still something!"

It was the conductor. He'd turned around.

This little man in his gray canvas jacket, thin, pale, with rotten teeth, had turned around, and his life is all he has; ten years, that's a lot for him.

Someone answers:

"What can you do?"

And they start spouting their wisdom, while a tree quickly passes over us, then another, and another, all along the tram's wire,—then one of them says:

"The only difference is that we'll go together, instead of going alone."

And another:

"Maybe it's even better this way, who knows?"

He laughs, he puffs on a small pipe that draws badly, his hand is behind him, around the iron rod barring the entrance to the platform: their wisdom, is it because of their age?

The man with the small pipe laughs again, shrugs his shoulders...

And suddenly, we can see there are a lot of people standing

in front of the station. There is a great change in front of the station. Endless rows of automobiles, almost doubled in height by the mountains of luggage, come to a halt in front of the ticket hall. A train whistle rose high above the dome of the central pavilion, and then fell down again, as when you suddenly cut off a water jet. It's the hour of the morning express trains: the express train to Simplon, the express train to the Bernese Oberland; you would think people are escaping to the mountains. And yet the postmen are still in their little group on the square, carrying, in a pile before them, parcels of publications held together by strings and reaching just under their chins. The postmen board the tram. There must have been around ten of them. And the last one, apologizing for the inconvenience:

"You should have seen those trains! It was something else! We had to fight for a seat. There were people clinging to the steps of the wagons!..."

It's clear that things are in motion. The tram also. The conversation continues. The tramway bell, the cars, the trucks, the avenue; and the oldest of the postmen, a paunchy man with small rivers beading drop by drop over the big tufts of his eyebrows:

"They say it will go up one degree each day ..."

"Yes."

"93° today, 95° tomorrow, 97° ... 113° ... 200° ... Hell!"

No Speaking to the Conductor: the rules are respected here; you do not speak to him, he speaks to you.

As the tram goes up the wide avenue, there the conductor goes again, he turns around with his worry and the little black mustache on a face pale as ash:

"Where did you read that?... For God's sake!"

He taps his heel violently to sound the bell.

Jackets are unbuttoned over cotton flannel shirts, themselves open, chests put at ease. There is the movement of a hand as it pushes back a cap, there is this cluster of people being swayed from the front to the back, from the back to the front by the car's motion;—there is a laugh, there is the man with the pipe; the man with the pipe resumes:

"We'll be in good company."

He laughs.

A stop. Two or three postmen get off. A new avenue. And this is when we saw police officers already stationed in front of the National Bank.

VIII

One man came, then another. It hatched inside of you. This man, waking well before dawn, had thought: "What if it were true! What if it all disappears!"

And that's how it went. Instead of thinking: "And my money too ... oh well!" he saw only his money, and he wanted to stop it from disappearing.

That's how it went. Only this consolation. Only this child, but the most beloved of the children, the most pampered, the most groomed, the one who weighed the most in your arms and against your heart,—your money.

And so, one man came, then another, then another, and so police were stationed in front of the bank and a crowd started gathering behind the line of officers.

The billposter also came. In the front pocket of his smock the black-and-white text is folded in four; he is holding his glue pot. The snake charmer's bare leg on the right had been glued on and, on the left, the title of a play that was meant to be touring, but everyone had already stopped worrying about such things.

Right in the middle of what is there, on top of whatever, without taking into account anybody's rights, quickly: the man, grabbing the poster, affixes it from two of its corners, smoothing it out flat with a brush.

And so, the people came; they began to read what was written.

It was a proclamation from the State Council; how strange! The government was appealing to its citizens' common sense: and it is precisely what should reassure you that scares you. There are those images inside us: we can already no longer stop the outside from looking like the images, having been influenced by them. A fear has hatched inside of you; everything heightens it. It makes you hold your head differently, gives your face a different color; it is painted on your face, the fear passes from your face to the face of the person you've just met. No sooner seen than shared. Where man has not intervened nothing in particular has yet been written, not above the rooftops, nor on the eight sides of the steeple, nor where those blends are found among the leaves, those sweet blends of a little air, sun, dust, and a black color, that of the branches. It's in a heart, a first heart. In a head with short or long hair, that is to say where there is consciousness, and the feeling that everything with a beginning has an end. And well, what if this is the end!

As for me, I was not so sure anymore. This morning, having come, having boarded the tram, having been brought by it to the central kiosk, among the pigeons painted by the messengers: green and brown, yellow and pink, blue. Are those around me going faster or am I giving them this speed? This different pace. All those people coming, and those little local gentlemen with their grave and cold expressions of tranquil people who can imagine nothing beyond themselves,—completely changed, approaching each other, gesturing to each other. They are here, they are here still—and I, for my part, standing beneath this never-before-experienced power of the sun with its new color, as every line of the rooftops trembles; then, addressing it: "Burn! Inflict pain, intensify!" I am here, I stand here, I am forced to stand here. I arrived, in the middle of this considerable thing, and I am not

33

sure whether it is inside of me or outside of me. There are firemen passing with their copper-crested helmets and heavy waist belts. Nine o'clock chimes: the nine strokes roll over you like crumbling blocks of stone, falling one after the other with a sound louder than the other sounds.

We turn to the sun: "Are you there?" It is still there.

And there is still this threat of the end, but without our knowing when the end will intervene, upon or between which of the twelve black-and-white Roman numerals high above us, with the hand moving at the same speed from one number to the other;—without our being able to read when the end will occur, neither on this fabricated sun, nor on the real one: and so there is only a great reflection of the end cast upon all things, as when the star itself tilts.

It was as if the star were setting, the interior star, interior to you, with a new color, with a new kind of light: upon things, upon all things, upon the women with bare arms passing by ...

IX

A voice was heard:

"Are they scared, or what?... The others are. Not us!"

Then:

"They're all running away! Well, good riddance!"

It's coming from the poor neighborhoods.

"We'll stay right where we are, this'll be good for us. I'm telling you: If everything goes up in flames, all the better for us!..."

The accordion then makes another attempt, from behind the glass, where a mug overflowing with foam is seen upside down, showing its beautiful white and beautiful brown:

"That's not it!"

The man was in the corner; and the man who was across from the man with the accordion:

"That's not it; you haven't got it yet! You've got to change it up a little. Today, change it up, now that everything's changing ... Faster!... That's it!... Go!"

He himself began to sing.

He himself had begun to sing, having entered the music through a small entrance, and had run with it;—then one table, then two, come into view behind the dirty glass, where the muslin curtains hang, mended many times over.

There, in those poor neighborhoods, those low neighborhoods, at that end of the city; in between the hills, where no one goes anymore, where everything is a secret, is badly lit; where the city hangs heavy with all its might, all its weight, preventing the day from descending, preventing the air from circulating;—and a man plays the accordion and another sings, because he'd said: "Freedom!"

From now on, we are free, equal!

On the left and the right, a succession of low black facades with their shops: the ragpicker, the furniture dealer, the old-iron merchant; and that's how it goes, down each side of the alley, off toward other alleys just like it: a whole tangle of alleyways, knotted into each other, as though a little cat had scrambled a ball of yarn.

Here, in this fold between two hills, the low city and the low life; in these underworlds, these lower regions, these prisons;— here, all of a sudden, freedom!

First there was one here, just one man, as if the thing was written only for this one man who first read it;—and who reread it aloud.

"Now nothing can stop us from doing whatever we want, you hear me, all of you, from now on, nothing ... But let's hurry up!"

Reading it once more: "Hey you, go on, the accordion!"

"It's not like that, like what he said, today everything changes."

And the accordion starts up again; and then the other starts singing.

Little by little, it starts to rise; something rises from beneath and between the rooftops.

From above we heard it, without yet understanding exactly what it was, this thing that was coming. Something was making its way to us, something we did not see coming. Behind those doors still shut tight, on the other side of those walls; beneath tiles the color of overcooked bread, black with soot, green with moss.

There where we stood and had been standing until now;—but some shutters swung open, followed by more; a woman: "Let's go!" and the wooden staircases resound beneath their hobnailed shoes.

The man stopped singing.

"Whatever we want, and however we want it, so let's go!"

He sees people coming, he sees people entering. He raises his glass: "It doesn't cost a thing anymore, it won't ever cost a thing again!" And they don't really understand yet, but they will be made to understand.

"Hey! All of you, come in! Listen up, we're going to explain ..."

And a silence; then the noise starts up again.

Muffled, from below. We still cannot really make it out, we still do not really understand it. As when the hail clouds would loom, do you remember, on certain August days, over the vineyard; when the hailstorm had not yet fallen, when it had not yet passed the mountain. Before we could see anything, when at the edge of the sky there was only this white cloud, like a bedsheet.

And also, this sound, this very sound. As when troops are on the march, as when large numbers of men are on their way.

X

"It's extremely hot, don't you think?"

Both of them are on their boat; there's Panchaud the elder, and the other one.

Here, nothing yet but the water, still the same, and the great heat over that water, and the boat they are both in, Panchaud Édouard and his brother Jules.

Having said something, Panchaud Édouard then said nothing further. Jules didn't even respond.

The water says nothing either. Silence on all sides, here; nothing speaks. Smooth and flat wherever you turn, the lake reaches the vineyards in the north, the mountain to the south. And between this north and south, nothing, nowhere, just water, a silent water; never before so silent, it seems, never so stingy with words and phrases, with its enormous thickness carrying only a boat on its back, harboring its fish, that's all:—when we're here, facing the open water; and the gulf, painted on its shoreline with overturned poplars, offers you only this vastness, deprived of meaning and lacking in scale.

The two Panchaud brothers are lying down inside their boat. We hear strikes against iron, but it's as if we cannot not hear it. The mechanical saw is like a big buzzing bee, but as if the bee has hovered too long in the air. Afternoon, three in the afternoon, perhaps; but there is no time, because there is no change.

They could forge in the smithy all they wanted, they could shoe a horse brought to them, they could finish shoeing it, and start shoeing another; the carpenter in his cool little workshop could plane as much as he wanted, pushing the plane with both hands to the end of a first board, a second board, a third board:—it only happened later, when Édouard Panchaud stood up.

We looked again, we did not recognize ourselves. There is a man before us; everything changes. Cooked, cooked again, black and brown with gleams on his ribs, and, when the skin is taut, some areas completely white, with pants loosely fastened around his waist:—Panchaud, Panchaud Édouard, and all it took was for him to stand.

First the head, then a shoulder, then the other shoulder. Panchaud Édouard, or any one of us. From within and below, a force was at play. He does not know; he knows nothing. He is nothing, he is nothing but a man, but any man was enough. The most precious thing. The man was lying down, now he stands. We watch him grow little by little against the mountain and surpass it. He organizes everything on each side of his person. It said nothing, it meant nothing, it did not exist, it had all been empty;—a meaning had now come to everything.

Still, right? This man is still here to make us feel how necessary he is, so that we miss him even more later on. That just one man still be here,—before he vanishes. That just one man grow in stature little by little; and, now, watch how he commands his arms and makes them move, tracing an immense circle on distant rocks, on deserted skies; and now the rock comes alive and the sky is repopulated. Panchaud, feeling thirsty, had risen: with both hands, he grabbed the black bottle his brother handed him and he drank, bringing it to his mouth. Drinking up there, his mouth open. The mouth of the bottle does not touch his lips. The thin stream of water now exiting the bottle is forced to trace a visible path through the air. Panchaud drinks, and everything begins again. Then a song rises in the forge, the plane begins to laugh and grunt. The saw starts a long and whistling scale, ascending to the end. There is no longer just one boat, there are two; one that is pale green, the other, overturned, dark green. And on top of it, in the middle of it all, there is Panchaud standing, dangling one mountain to one side, another mountain to the other side. He is like a porter bearing a double load, a carrier of burdens who knows how to distribute his burdens, is in no way hindered by his burdens. He is like a fairground strongman surrounded by his weights, smiling among his weights. At some point, he stretches his arm out: he carries the mountain peak five feet from him, he barely bends his neck. He is like Samson in the Bible, when Samson broke the columns with his hands, making them crumble.

XI

Meanwhile the cavalry and the machine gunners had been assembled. There was, here as elsewhere, in the early days, this military diversion. A word had passed from mouth to mouth: revolution; and now all anyone saw was that threat, which had come to the fore. There are those who have and those who do not: the latter, in the early days, seemed to have prevailed without difficulty. Freedom; yes, but how to grab hold of it? The noise hanging in the air hushed; listen! we hear nothing now, or just that they're having fun. Today, a weekday, in those poor neighborhoods, it's like a Sunday. All the cafés are full, and there are many people in the streets: a Sunday, like a Sunday, a national holiday, — as when there were holidays, as when there was still a calendar and holidays inscribed in that calendar. All these people in their Sunday clothes, all those Italian masons passing by arm in arm, the day laborers, their wives, their children, the families. The old people no one has seen for months because they don't go out anymore, — and who were suddenly brought outside, and who were now helped to walk, some crippled, some paralyzed. The big women wearing faces full of makeup, their heads bare, their hair dyed yellow as was the fashion some twenty years ago, their feet in slippers, nothing but a blouse covering their bodies: it's so hot out! We go to check the thermometer. Ah! That's right! We had forgotten. And we quickly headed for the shade, and we headed for the fountains; and we headed for all kinds of shade and refreshments. At the Bras de Fer café, there is a big room for dancing: and so some were dancing, after dropping a ten-cent coin in the orchestrion. And in the other neighborhoods, the bourgeois neighborhoods, there too the most crucial thing had been forgotten, because the general mood was one of intense relief. Most men are made in such a way that they can only pay attention to the present moment, to trivialities; they like to be fooled. Few raise their eyes to the sky, few understand it. Few know even of its existence, that great mechanism there above, the star that is somewhat close, the star getting closer still.

Now they watched the cavalry squadrons passing by on their big horses, handsome boys from the countryside, their faces red under their nickel-plated shako chains, their muskets hanging from their saddles, their cartridge belts in bandoliers; and they watched the infantrymen standing on trucks, with their steel helmets painted gray,—as in Ancient Greece, thinks the middle school teacher, as in one of Homer's songs, when they laid siege to Troy;—decidedly, society was standing firm. Then came the applause, the men lifting their hats, the women waving their hands,—among the muffled rumble of large reinforced tires, the large rubber and leather tires with their gleaming spikes.

On the square, all the pigeons flew away.

The helmeted heads and their shoulders were seen once more in front of the church-side fountain, with its scarlet geraniums and the column above;—they suddenly emerged from the shadows, entering that immense well of light that the eye was climbing, attempting to climb all the way to the opening up above, but could not ...

Because it is 100° today beneath this blazing sky, we try to escape;—and so, more than ever, on all those paths descending to the lake, the infinite troop of swimmers.

Some, the moment they are undressed, run to the end of the diving platform and throw themselves in, headfirst. We hear the sound, we see the splash, we see rings form.

Many heads float like fishing bobbers on the water, with its lighter and darker patches.

There are perfectly smooth areas and then others where, for some strange reason (given that there is no wind) a fizzing of sorts appears, a gentle bubbling, like oil in a frying pan.

The lack of waves, along with the heat, had made the moss abound. Here is the lake, the lake beside the city: the sun comes to drink, the sun slurps at its straw, with two lips the sun comes, steadily slurping: and so we see how the different species of algae have grown massively, rising from the depths in forests of great height, and careless swimmers trip over their peaks. Never such a drought, never such a heat: but never, either, had there been so much water. Never, as the regulars say, the anglers, the fishing netmen, the boaters; never, they said, never ever. In the early days, it had rapidly retreated, it had gone in reverse, having dropped several feet along the gently sloping shores, revealing a large strip,—and that had been the beginning. And the drought had continued; yet we could see that the waters were rising again, as if on a gentle impervious tide. The water had begun to bathe the walls of the quay it had abandoned, it had once again covered the large rim of sand, hard as cement, which it had left bare; it had pushed even further, going where it never had before, to the path bordering the shore, to the acacia bushes, to the weeping willows, sloshing into their trunks through holes,—rising, rising still, up to where? And, yes, it's like a tide, but made by what moon? we ask ourselves. And then, suddenly, we understood. This same sun that takes, gives. The sun takes from one place; in another, it gives. It removes, but it supplies. And what had happened was, finally, that it had supplied more than it had removed, thanks to the enormous input from glaciers and the Rhône, the Rhône that was swollen, bloated and overflowing, which had become like milk. Over there, the input was still infinitely larger than what was borrowed, the whole mountain coming down through its torrents; and so, again: up to where? Up to where? the fishermen ask each other in their backlit boats, men who, in a string of black figures, look like telegraph alphabet symbols.

Here is the lake shore. Let us name everything here. Let us name only what is here. There are the fishing boats, not far from the large brown hangars of the Compagnie Général de Navigation shipyards, black and white smokestacks looming over the rooftops, and in the background, the mountain the color of a grocery bag:—we climb back up to the city. In the irrigated meadow, the farmhand walks alongside a red horse bending its neck toward a ditch full of greasy water; a man, lying under a tree, arms crossed, looks dead. There are flies everywhere; there are barns with red doors. The strong smell of manure bars your way like a wall. Now the villas, the city commences. Rental properties spread out before you on all sides, soon meld together. The train station's location is marked by smoke; we glimpse, higher up, the post office buildings and the banks.

Torpor, silence. It's difficult to move. The few people who are out pause beneath trees, remove their hats, grab their handkerchiefs. There are hardly any children, only in the passageways between houses. An assembly has come together carrying fasces on the train station square. We keep climbing. Suddenly, we hear drums.

Place Saint-François, the same day, in the evening; it's all they could find. They seem to still be having fun; it's just one more diversion, a way to pass the time. They have formed a procession; in the front are the drums. Then men who are completely drunk, women shouting. The men hold on to each other to keep from falling. Around six; everyone goes to their windows. The shopkeepers step out on the sidewalks; many people join the parade.

A patrol on the other side of the square, however, takes swift action.

Arm in arm. The afternoon promenade continues; only now, they have left their neighborhoods, they have come to see how things are elsewhere; there has been some kind of progression.

They have started to sing "L'Internationale."

They speak of epidemics breaking out. All the hospitals are full. Passersby are falling dead in the streets.

And then: "What is happening?"

And then, suddenly: "Ah! So it's true!"

XII

She had made herself beautiful to please him, she had done her hair the way he liked.

She had set the table herself, bringing out the blue china, as if guests were coming to visit.

There were flowers in a vase; in a bowl, fruits of the season. There were also fruits which had ripened, that year, well ahead of the season: black figs, white figs, apples, and pears.

He had come as he did every other night, at the same time. He had pretended like nothing was different. Everything had been as usual. He had come, they had sat across from each other; they had started to eat. Through the window they could see the beautiful sunset happening behind the trees. Night fell, they had turned on the lamp. A dinner like any other. Together like before; together, on that night, once more.

But suddenly he wonders, "Together?"

He looks at her, he sees her there, and he is there; and that makes two. I thought we were one, but I was wrong.

Suddenly, he realizes. Oh! You whom I chased for so long, I will still not have reached you, because two is not enough, and there are two of us.

Two is not satisfying, two irritates, two is miserable, two means no, two is a contradiction, two is the destruction of one by one; I thought we were but one: we are two, we will remain two.

There are perhaps just a very few days left, after that everything will be finished: and she will go her way, and I will go mine. Even if it's in the same time, in the same place, because she will continue to be outside of me and I outside of her. We will be taken separately, one and one. He sees, in advance, how it will be. And so, having seen it, it's as if he is seeing her, too, for the first time. What was hidden has come into view, what was at the surface vanishes, being there only as ornament; being only flesh and flesh vanishes. She who is there will be disrobed twice, she who will not be me, she who will not have been me ...

In the silence of the evening, big butterflies, covered in a thick gray dust, which made no sound as they flew, had entered; they kept bumping into the wallpaper lampshade, they fell on the tablecloth. We feel something extraordinary happening; sleep vanishes from the earth and abandons the inside of men's heads. There is the smell of warm walls, the smell of gunflint, which is also a taste on your lips. Continuously, the garden creaks: it's the ground retreating to different cores of contraction, like the muscles of the body that each have their own connection point. The beams jerk playfully beneath the weight of the roof tiles;—and she has lied to me, and she lies to me, she lies to me completely, without knowing it, just because she is, just by being.

Watching, watching again as the bone beneath flesh, a negation of what is above it, comes forth; and, suddenly, what is pleasing, what is sweet, what is silken, what is painted in beautiful colors, shaded in shapes, what is embellished with lines, is only there for a little while, like when you put the tablecloth on the table, like tonight's flowers in their vases, like Sunday clothes that will have to be taken off at some point.

This is how it still was for this man, on that night, and the man was in front of the woman he loved and accused her. She

47

lied to me, I lied to myself, everything lied to me. Love lies, O dear beloved! Distance is coming between us, space is coming, time is coming, more space still, more time still. He sees her drift off like a boat drifting off,—growing smaller, more uncertain, less distinct, becoming a black dot, which has not signaled, not even waved,—which is no longer anything ...

And, suddenly, returning to himself.

Returning to himself: "No! it's not possible!... You're not lying, you can't lie, love can't lie; forgive me!"

He called to her. He calls to her, he says: "Give me your hand, I don't know what happened, it's only perhaps that we didn't love each other enough, love can do anything, and so let it; let the world go, little one, let it happen; you're here, all is well ..." Returning to himself.

We heard the earth cracking again in the garden.

Ah! No! Your hand cannot lie to me, because the path is through your hand, through one of your arms, through all of you;—he held her against him, once more he was drawn to her.

He could no longer see a thing, the world had vanished. The outside world has vanished, but it is because I hold a bigger, more beautiful world. A world where I am not alone, a world where I am no longer two;—when he grabbed her like that, he carried her off with him, he held her so close, as if to make her enter him, as if to break through ...

And so it went for a moment; then went back down again. As when a walnut, touching the ground, cracks in two. Unity, once more, where have you gone? I am two. He sees before him this great surface of flesh again. He says: "I don't love you!" he says: "You are nothing!" He screams. He screams: "You're the enemy!" He says nothing, there is no sound, he has not moved, she does not move. "Go away!" He says nothing; he screams. Does she hear him? Is she pretending not to hear him? When he sees now all of the space she occupies;—she who is only a hindrance, a thing that you are constantly bumping into then having to speak to, when you should be pushing her away, because she is all lies, she is the wrong path, and elsewhere, there is the right one;—she who prevented him from seeing it, who is too great a mass, who is a substantial body, because she is always ahead and in front, depriving you of seeing, of seeing yourself ...

"Go away!" And perhaps there is still time.

And then, suddenly, once more, returned, not knowing anymore; seeking this body by hand, still and again, pressing it to her, this body allowing it, this body yielding little by little and crumbling toward him at its edges, like an embankment;—there is no in use in pretending, right? Take refuge there, make yourself small, allow it to happen; merely move your head to that warm crevice, and say nothing more;—I'll stay right here, put your hand in mine, like this; I am at peace ... And now death can come, because all is well, because all is sweet.

When the great body of a woman is around us,—like wool, like cloth, like a blanket, like the warm nest around a bird's babies.

XIII

I listen to the arrival of the sounds as they once were, as they arrive now.

While I still can, I listen, and it's as if they still arrive, still arise, as they did in the times before. In the middle of the night, a train whistled. We could hear the conductor's horn. We could hear the sound of cars bumping one another in a succession of thuds all along the train, in a night full of life. Around midnight, half past midnight, the train took a drink; it whistled, sputtered, coughed. I listen.

Tonight, I listen, and there's nothing left, whichever way I turn, searching even the nooks and crannies of the air, as if with a broom.

In each nook, each cranny, every corner of the air: nothing.

From their little brick sentry boxes, with all those levers lined up behind them, each bearing an inscription of black letters on an enamel plaque, the switch operators near the switch box are waiting too, for something that does not come.

The 775 did not arrive, the 33 that should have followed did not arrive.

And now, the express from Simplon should have been announced; it wasn't ...

I loved the world too much; I see that I loved it too much. Now that it is going away. I became too attached to it, and I see now that it is detaching itself from me. I loved it completely, despite itself. I loved it despite its imperfections, completely,—because of its imperfections, having seen that only through these imperfections did perfection exist; and it was good because it was bad.

And all things came, all men came. I was no longer able to choose between things; I was no longer able to choose between men. Although I knew things well; although I knew men well, having seen them as they were, which is to say small, ugly, mean,—or not even ugly, or mean: mediocre, formless, only half-born, not inhabiting their form, unexpressed. And I sought to keep them away from me at first, but they came, more came still, so many came!

On a wooden shelf near the door, underneath a brass weight, are sheets of paper of various colors: schedules, diagrams, service orders: they have read them, they will reread them, then nothing.

They look everywhere they can: nothing. Before them is the bulge of the rails, like a swollen muscle with its fibers visible. It shines because of the lanterns. It was useful for a long time, it is made to last even longer, it is ready, it waits,—and nothing, nothing comes anymore ...

I loved the world too much. When I sought to imagine something beyond it, it was still the world that I imagined. When I sought to go past it, there I found it again. I tried closing my eyes to see the heavens: it was Earth; and the heavens were the heavens only when they became Earth once again. When we began to suffer there once more, complain, question ourselves;—beneath trees like our trees, beneath seasons of trees and plants like ours, because summer is summer only when there was winter.

Existence, existence alone. That just one thing exists, whatever the thing, in whatever way. All of it. The four elements, the three kingdoms; minerals, plants, beasts; air, fire, earth, water. The

51

raised, the flat, the round, the sharp: what is beautiful is existence. All things: those with three dimensions, those with two, the real, the figurative, the real three-dimensional bodies and their two-dimensional imitations;—the imitations we made of them because we were not satisfied with them, because they simply were, and we wanted to have doubles of them, we wanted to have them even more to ourselves, we duplicated them, we merged with them, we no longer know where we end, where they begin. And so I found myself with a taste for everything, no preference, I don't know how, I can't really explain it (even now, reaching for exactly that, to tell it one more time, tell it to myself one last time, tell everything and tell myself), even now ... And then, nothing ...

There is the train station farther on. There is that enormous hall lit up from below by electric moons: wide open to allow entry, always entry after entry, where nothing enters anymore. Along a walkway are colorful lights whose colors have not changed, though normally they change continuously: green, purple, red, white. Something has stopped beating in the arteries of the world; the world is vanishing: I loved it too much.

Since I was unable to choose, still I go to its riches, still I attempt to make a quick choice and cannot;—attempting then to jump out of the world,—unable to, even now, trapped by my feet, brought back to where I should be, to my rightful place. Dear bodies, poor bodies, magnificent bodies, O matter! Matter of the five senses, tasteable, visible, touchable, inhaled, heard, caressed, savored, I attract all that to me still, despite myself, through all my windows of flesh.

It is impossible that it will be taken from us; it is impossible that all of creation was created for nothing.

All these raw or processed materials; the good artisan's table, the love he put into it. The love he expended into it and into the stone he sculpted. There was love before, it cannot be that there is no love after. It cannot be that there is not love always. That all of it would vanish, that all of it would be as if it had never been! Quickly, I flash back through time; and I tell myself: love, I see all that we have loved. It couldn't have all been lies, could it? Flash back, quick, remember the old times, when we climbed through the vineyards. The walls stained green with sulfate, the stakes gray like stone. The bottle of white wine, the big glasses on the table painted brown, a pipe nearby, and, near the pipe, a pack of tobacco. The good things, the beautiful things; this earth, and its sky. We watched the weather come in from over the Jura, because on that day, it was from over the Jura that the wind came and lifted its staff to drive the flock of its clouds. All these things that we loved. And then it'll be as if it hadn't ever been. So much love, then as if no love. That day, and then as if that day never happened. And not only that day, but also all those days of before;—as if there had been no days at all, because there would be no more days hereafter.

All that was said, all that was done, all that had been thought, recited, formulated, fashioned, modeled, built: so much love doled out and then love would be no longer. And they lived to express it, and then they would no longer express themselves, ever again. For, all at once, they would turn mute forever, having spoken for so long, having lived for so long surrounded by the sound of their speech; and then, silence. As if they'd never said a thing, as if they had always been lying on their backs in a corner, hands together, feet together, all along.

Silence and night everywhere. Over what lies behind, over what lies ahead. Over Assyria and over Egypt, the Indies and us, Greece and us. Over Rome. And over you too, beautiful France, mother of good workers of all kinds and in every field;—yet turned forever idle, forever out of work, people who have never been out of work!

Even so, they continue to exist, those two, in their high brick tower with the window; coming and going across the floor, with footsteps that resound as on the deck of a ship.

They come and go, continuing to search all over, never finding anything. Going east, then west. Going north, consulting the north: "And you, what about you?"

Then toward the southeast, where the lake is, and where the water is, henceforth uninhabited, before a mountain that is uninhabited, which itself stands below an uninhabited sky.

There were, on that night, far too many stars that were too white. Everyone is left alone with their questions; everything has stopped. They are naked on their beds, everywhere; they toss and turn, they seek a place for their heads. Naked, having removed everything including the nightshirt bothering them, but there is another bother which is in the air, which is the air. Everyone fights for their life,—constantly beating back something they want to keep away from them, which is them, which is their own skin, how they are made, the real threat they pose to themselves—with each hand, with both feet, with gestures slow or sudden. Using precaution or, on the contrary, violence. The small children, the mothers, the young, the old. In the thickness of the air, on the sheets. Under a roof or under no roof; in every one of these hundreds and hundreds of houses alongside each other, spread out or in clusters, with windows lit up or unlit,—the old, the young, the rich, the poor, the sick, the healthy.

For there is no longer any difference between them.

XIV

Hello anyway!

Hello things, all things! Hello, country! This country here.

I will once more let my imagination bring me over the water, standing at the foot of the mainmast, under the sail outstretched like a pregnant woman's belly, and then:

"Hello!"

Climbing one last time on one of those big boats transporting stones, with the black hull, standing on its thick, rough floor, like a road's surface, watching the mountain come to me slowly; and:

"Hello! Hello, you there in front of me, you there above me!"

I doffed my hat:

"Hello, gentlemen of Lavaux!"

We've said hello to the Savoyards opposite, and now we come your way. We've crossed the lake again. We come beneath the two big sails, green and soaked in sulfate, or in ocher and then russet, beneath one or the other, at the foot of the mainmast, and we're here, after over there.

Hello to you we make our way to, and you who are on your way, we see you from afar as you work, we recognize you by your walls long before we've spotted you: all this construction on its way, with its progress and its gulfs, this great slope men made by hand, excavated, sculpted, carved by men, entirely rebuilt by men, with its levels and steps, its superimpositions of terraces and

55

degrees: and hello anyway! you over there, because you've worked, hello, come what may!—When we see you, and when we come, turning and changing direction all the time, then the mountain, too, turns each time and it's the mountain (not us) that seems to turn; it presents one side, then the other;—but only presents, presents, and represents, we can't get enough of it.

Oh! How many walls there are, and yet how those walls encouraged each other, those walls over there! When we come, we look, we get closer, we get closer still, and now we can start to count.

Hello, hello, anyway! you who raised these walls!

When we arrive, when we see it, that quarter mile of sheer coastline, which without you would have long since fallen into the water and collapsed, and without you the whole coast would have long since come down, but you were there,—so, hello! Hello to you and regards to you!

In my imagination, I stand on the boat coming in from the open water and try to count: walls more than seven hundred feet high and nearly ten miles long,—and how many can there be of these little floors, these stone cases and boxes, these beginnings of rooms set one beside the other, set one above the other, progressing, retracting, extending outwards into corners, hollowed out into gulfs, all shaped, sculpted by man, arranged in semicircles, which are concave, then convex, and from afar as smooth and uniform to the eye as velvet, then abruptly thwarted with their green and gray checkerboards, the disorder of their checkerboards, their tumbling down the slope, as when a dump truck is unloaded at the bottom of an embankment;—oh! how many there are! and, again:

"Hello!"

Greeting these walls again, and it's the work of men I greet as it comes into view,—how men have carved the immense coast in their image, having had an idea, having realized it through time and the ages, from generation to generation, without allowing themselves to stop ...

I doff my hat:

"I salute you! and salute you anyway, gentlemen of Lavaux!

"Hello, gentlemen of today! And I do mean gentlemen of today, and not just those from before,—because it wasn't enough to build, you had to keep building, maintain, conserve; it wasn't enough to do, you had to redo; it was falling apart, it was coming down, it was always being mined, worked; the whole slope was coming down; so you were masons, you were not just winegrowers, you became masons, you hauled up the earth, you hauled it up after every winter in sacks on your backs, from bottom to top, all of it; you were diggers, engineers, contractors, architects, laborers, whatever you could do, and however you could do it;—and, thanks to you, it held up, it endured!

"So, hello again and anyway! Come what may, I salute you for your work, even before you have shown yourselves."

For they do show themselves today, I can see that now. They are no longer showing themselves; no one does. We greeted them, we called to them, they do not answer.

They are no longer there, or if they are, you can't see them. In the overly bright day, the overly great day, the overly intense heat, all so discouraging, they have not come out, or they are lying flat at the foot of their walls, lying down in a row, if there are several of them, in the narrow shadow of the wall, the very thin strip of shade as when we underline a word in black ink, and they are lying there, and no longer move.

And me, as I arrive:

"Hello anyway!"

The greeting goes unanswered, no matter, I doffed my hat:

"Hello, you in front of me! And hello, you above me!—despite everything, and come what may."

XV

We're off. This is only a small image, though; this is a crew working on a drain on the road, not far from a bridge.

The stream, which used to chatter a great deal under the bridge, had stopped speaking for several days.

One of the men had gone all the way to the parapet, then, leaning over, had looked, and seen the stones. Only stones now. Everything had been drunk, it's over. He had returned with his empty bottle.

It was that seventh or eighth day; they had resumed work for the last time, that morning. They had gone to the large crate, locked by a padlock to which the supervisor had the key; they had taken off their jackets, many even their shirts, leaving on only their pants, and a small black leather belt around their waists.

They were gradually digging the ditch.

The man farthest ahead marked the edges with two pick marks; the man behind him blew up the tarmac; it was only the man behind that one who started digging. Order still prevails. They had been placed at equal distances one behind the other. The sky was white, a strange white. In the early morning, they had seen it as if from behind a thick white veil. The men were of many colors, of all ages; a heavy man was next to a thin man, a young man next to an old man; some were short, some were very tall. There were these external differences which are internal differences, which divide you. They continued as best they could, they continued all morning, then they ate, each having brought his own provisions in a bag or a basket. They had sat by the stream which had lost its voice, its songs, its stories; over them, too, a great silence had fallen.

It's this new kind of silence, this silence that noise no longer disperses or animates. Them, within it. And they still moved their jaws, but they weren't even moving their hands, placed between their knees. Without saying anything, without thinking. Fatigue weighs on the things inside your head, like a paperweight on papers. They eat, then drink. And separately. From time to time, a car, after blaring its horn and slowing down, would pass by, or a horse-drawn carriage: then we saw the dust rise with difficulty, like silt at the bottom of a pond, and almost immediately fall back onto the grassy roadside, which was as white as the road and merged with it. At one o'clock, the supervisor blew his whistle. Those who were lying down began to sit up; those who were already seated stretched and yawned. They rubbed their eyes with one hand, then the other. Then they said, "Let's go!" one after the other, having risen; then, slowly and dragging their feet, they reclaimed their places, having picked up their tools which they had thrown onto the embankment. They could barely see each other, because the light was too bright and white, no longer a help to seeing, but a hindrance, and they were black inside of it. A solitary pick sounded; you had to wait a moment for the second to come, or for the tearing sound made by the blade of the shovel as it sank into the density of pebbles. And so on. For a little while longer.

A man arrived from elsewhere. They, alone, could not have made it happen.

Here, too, there was only one man at first, who arrived from elsewhere and walked along the road. We did not see him descending the road. We did not immediately notice when he stopped. We did not immediately hear when he called.

He had to keep coming, keep getting closer. This was the beginning.

First in one place, then in another, and then everywhere:

"Hey!"

This man who comes lifts his arm:

"Hey, can you hear me?"

A member of the crew stands up, a second does the same. And then, the man, again:

"Drop those tools! It's all over now!"

They were leaning, over there, with both hands on the handle of their pick or pickax: at some point, it begins. An idea presents itself to you, and you must first fasten it to the ones you already have, which you do awkwardly, as when your big fingers are too clumsy for a thin thread. Tie the knot, tie a first knot, and finally the knot is in place. And the man who had come, at that moment:

"But first, let's have a drink!"

He lifts his arm again toward the others, who may not yet have fully understood, beckoning them to come along;—and already each of them feels that there's something in them that was not there before. They were alone, now they are many. All together, they turn their heads. And all together: "Sure," without saying it, "but who's going to pay?" The man, as if he had heard them:

"We don't pay anymore, we'll never pay again! We drink for free. Nothing costs anything ..."

A shift is underway. In the white day, in this fog, in this mist, in this steam that tastes as bland as when you're doing the laundry, their heads go first, their shoulders follow. They moved one behind the other, having crossed the bridge, made of stone, with a single arch, over no water at all now, between withered ash trees, all leaning, gray alders, clumps of yellowed meadowsweet, each one causing the masses of air to tumble around him like clods. A few steps away, above a terrace, was a café hidden behind pruned chestnut trees. Suddenly, we saw the curtain hanging in the doorframe: that was not the hindrance. There are things we suddenly understand: the hindrance was not outside of us, it was inside us. It has vanished. We didn't dare, we lacked direction. It wasn't the curtain that blocked us from entering; this nothing, this piece of cotton cloth, weightless in the hand, easy to lift; it wasn't the arm, it was what commands the arm that was blocked. Fortunately, someone had come along, and he entered first. They entered behind him. They saw the tables unoccupied. They saw that the tables were unoccupied as if they had been waiting for them;—at that moment, a noise started to rise from the city, as they entered;—while the man banged on the table with his fist, and said to the owner:

"The best you've got and as much as you can carry."

It seems that the owner, too, has sensed the difference between now and before; he has gone pale.

He stands in the doorway of the kitchen from which he has just emerged; he had not even thought to close the door behind him.

"Drinks, you hear! Drinks and some food …"

And the man, counting:

"For thirteen people."

The owner made a gesture.

He made a gesture with his head; he returned to where he had come from. And, meanwhile, they take their seats, dragging the benches, pulling the stools to them, sitting close to each other with their elbows touching, while a great gaiety swept over them, and a strength, too.

The boss had reappeared. He steeled himself, he stiffened, he held out against his fear; he said:

"It's three francs a liter."

They laughed all together. There's no more need for direction. Now we know who we are.

"Okay! Go and get us some food first!"

Shouting this all together, while the owner stands there saying, "Money first!"

But they: "Are you going? No? Okay then!"

Two or three stand up.

Confusion. Already the wine, because it no longer costs anything, is not looked after. As a few of the men stood up, one of the liters spilled. Twelve or thirteen shouted, raising their arms in the darkness. Bare. Arms like beams, fists as big as their heads. On their backs, bulges of muscle like when cords end up in knots. Sweat runs down every part of their skin. They wipe their faces with their arms from hand to elbow. A stool topples. Flies swarm around them, and then fly up to take refuge on the ceiling. A loud noise is heard in the kitchen, where cupboards are being opened. What's in the cupboards is ours. It's all ours. And, because the owner is still protesting, they threw themselves at him, he struggled; now a table topples.

"Hold him! Yeah! That's it."

And then they shouted, "Let's tie him up!"

And, meanwhile, others had gone down to the cellar: and it didn't take long. Because everything is ours, everything is allowed. There was a barrel: instead of the men going down to fill jugs, wouldn't it be better to bring it up, and instead of going to the wine, what if the wine came to us? Since everything has changed. Since everything is permitted. Since nothing is forbidden. And the three of them were already hoisting the barrel up the narrow, slippery staircase, with its flimsy steps, but it's amazing how sturdy we are, how strong we are, how easy it is.

Just then, the tiles began to tumble. Something heavy was knocked over in the kitchen. Where the key is missing, the door is forced open. To speed things up, they grabbed a wood-splitting mallet. That's it! As you destroy, you develop the taste for destruction for destruction's sake. Even before you get drunk on wine, because that is not the only kind of drunkenness. They had laid the barrel on a table, to pour the wine from the spigot; it was taking too long; they set the barrel upright, they smashed it, drank straight from it. Evidently, there is a greater pleasure than drinking.

And a more beautiful kind of work than making: unmaking. They weren't tired anymore.

The pictures on the walls, the cabinet filled with glasses, the pints in a row, the liquor bottles, the beer tap, the windows, the chairs, the benches. A woman was shrieking on the floor above, several men went up; the woman shrieked louder, the woman shrieked no more. And, somehow, at this point, the innkeeper, who had been tied up then pushed into a corner, found himself rid of his ropes; he was then seen hurling himself at those closest to him: and so then, too, it became clear that there is even more pleasure in another kind of destruction:—when blood flows.

Suddenly, the man called to them:

"They're going to need us, over there. Let's go!"

Over there meant the side of town where a great deal of smoke was rising; they said, "Let's go."

Having knocked down everything that could fall, having hastily piled up the chairs and tables in a corner, having doused them with kerosene ...

The air is heavy. We don't walk straight. It doesn't matter, we'll make a line. Arm in arm. They had taken a red bedsheet and tied it to a pole. We'll place it in the front; it will walk in front of us. To say what we want, to say who we are. They took off down the road toward town, while the inside of the café was burning. Suddenly, a flame shot from the window, which they saw, having turned around;—then they began to sing, each one singing a song of his own, but it became a song for all, and that was beautiful; having thus begun to sing, supporting one another, helping one another, pushing one another forward; being many, being but one,—and that was beautiful;—being many, being but one single being.

XVI

That afternoon, we heard, for the first time, coming from the town, the sewing-machine sound of a machine gun. It's in the town, on the north side, behind the hill. It's at that spot over there, which is one of innumerable spots: and, between these innumerable spots, there are empty spaces, places where nothing is happening yet.

On this shore of the lake, the only thing that happened was that we tried in vain, that night, to switch on the electricity. The only other thing that happened, long before the night came, was that all the doors found themselves shut tight and locked, while all of the paths, the avenues, and even the gardens between their walls became completely deserted. I take another good look at how things are here; and it's seven o'clock. In the west over the great wall, between the elder and plum tree, there is this great sky, but all in all nothing beyond the ordinary, except for the unusual density of the mist, which had gradually become like ripening wheat (that kind of wheat we call red wheat). I went up to the attic. On their zinc roofs, which now I saw from above, the laundresses, my neighbors, were still hanging their laundry as they did every night, clipping the top two corners of the white or colored laundry to the clothesline. Three beautiful girls. They raise their bare arms into the sky. The roof beneath them emitted a mist and made their entire bodies tremble, blurring the outline

65

of their legs and bodices, and the blots of laundry around them are like boiling milk: they continue to laugh, they continue to chatter. I cast my eyes farther. There too, all is calm. There is the curve of the shore, its visible tip, with poplars, and with the water: over there are still some people living calmly, in peace. They have enough to live on in their cellars, their attics, their barns; they go on assuring and reassuring themselves about their surroundings and each other; and, possessing something, they conspire to keep it. I imagine the two Panchaud brothers who have gone fishing again,—surely they went fishing again this afternoon, and this is the hour they return. The soup is prepared in kitchens, because the woman goes to the garden to pick her aromatic herbs, goes to the fountain, fills her pail, goes to her pot of butter or the lard she has rendered herself from the kidney fat of her pig,—to her potato provisions. There still, in the beautiful fog of the heat, surely the blacksmith strikes his iron and the carpenter pushes his plane in the strong smell of tobacco, which mingles with the smell of resin. And I, still turned toward that great big pit, like the one inside a seated woman's belly, I no longer know. Is it really true? Is it possible? But now day is waning, it has weakened, it pulls away;—and we saw coming, along with the sunset, a nasty greenish color, in front of which is a reflection that reaches all the way to the trees, all the way to the zinnias in the garden.

We know that it's now on the northern side that the sky is red.

That the sky is red; and another red.

They have not rung the fire bell. I listen, we no longer hear anything.

We hear only someone beating against the store's shutters, then yelling: it's the cobbler Perrelet.

He must be drunk as usual. And he has come, as usual, to fetch something for his supper, which he makes himself, as he does not have a wife; but he has found the grocery store closed. He gets angry, he calls, he shouts, he shouts louder.

No one answers him, no one moves. Perrelet is still shouting. The flames, in the sky, at that moment, must have grown: an entire row of poplars took on the color, and they seemed to be moving at their base, as when the wind is blowing. And still no one. Everyone has taken refuge at home. People must be, I think, in their kitchens. I take a look; among the trees, a few windows: they no longer have their old shape, their clear shape, well defined; they have no outlines, blinking here and there like eyes half-open. No more electricity. They sit packed in their kitchens, around a candle not fully snuffed out, or around a foul-smelling gas lamp, not having been lit for a while. They can no longer tell themselves apart, despite the love there. They seek each other out, with their eyes that aren't very useful anymore. Their chests lack confidence, because there is a lack of air there. A woman says to her husband:

"Go see if the door is locked."

He went to look, he says:

"It is, but if we can't go out tomorrow ..."

The woman opens the cupboard:

"There's still some stew."

She points to what's left of some beef stew on a plate; but the milk, tomorrow morning, what if the milkman doesn't come?

Then the man:

"We'll have to be like the others, we'll have to grab our guns."

And in the house next door, it was the same; in that other house the same; and then there is the third, where a man is alone with his child.

His wife is on a trip, the little maid is gone. He cooked himself, he had to think of it all. He had to be the same as always; there are many things you must remember in a home. He prepared the bath for the little one; he bathed him. And now, the little one laughs, claps his hands; he says: "Papa, why are they firing the cannon?" but before there is time to answer, he's already on to the next question.

A little light soup, a piece of toasted bread, fruit marmalade;—the boy came over. His legs are bare, he's wearing sandals, a sleeveless robe; he was seated at the table, his teddy bear was sat at his side.

Everything has to be taken care of, because to the little one everything still matters.

Everything that already doesn't matter to you anymore has to be taken care of, because that's what matters to him, not the rest, he doesn't know. He cannot see the differences, he carries on. In simplicity and also in truth, because he is innocent. But what about me ...

Night comes. The child was still very amused by the candle. Then he was tired. Suddenly, as on every night; he goes about his life. He carries on with his little life, without wondering until when.

He goes about as he pleases; he rubs his eyes, his head tilts. He will accept everything that comes, and that's beautiful;—but what about me?

The little bed was painted white; on the night table, a porcelain nightlight.

The cretonne curtains hung with folds in front of another kind of curtain, which was a great silence, and the air that is lifeless, suffocating, which sought a way in.

And the father placed the little one on his bed, but immediately the little one awoke. That's how it goes. Sleep comes to them, goes off, returns. Now he's thinking about his games. So free! So consistently a friend to himself and to everything, so well tuned to everything, no matter what happens,—because he won't know, because he won't defend himself, because he will never be able to do anything but accept it; he goes about in this way, with no lies;—and so, and so … My God! He's better than me. He's not the one who needs me, I'm the one who needs him!

And not able to resist, having approached the bed, having knelt down, his arms before him on the sheet …

"Papa, are you praying for me?"

Nothing, stillness. He's not really there anymore. He no longer does a thing, things are done for him. He remains completely calm so that things can be done properly; he doesn't interfere, is more and more and more trapped, is more and more inside;—while the child does what he's been taught to do: sit, clasp his hands, close his eyes.

And then came the words he believed in, only because they're there, as when the wind comes through a tree.

XVII

At the hotel, they had quickly gone to look for all the candles in storage, of which there were fortunately several boxes, and they'd arranged them themselves, most of the staff having already disappeared. They stood them up with wires, like Christmas tree candles, in the chandeliers and on the wall mounts. They also stuck them in the necks of empty bottles and placed one on every table. The women had dressed up. Everything seemed to be setting the stage for something that had not been permitted before, that's why. Once more, they had stood in front of their mirrors with their powders, their blush, and their pencils; once more, they had freshened themselves up, trying to be not what they were, but what they would have liked to be. Not being enough as they were, determined to be more. Constantly comparing the image in the mirror to the one they carry inside; seeing that their arms are white, but not white enough, their cheeks are rosy, but not rosy enough. Seeing red on their lips, they need to amplify it, add to it. And again tonight, more carefully tonight, meticulously, thoroughly. Then they arrived. Arms bare, neck bare, back, throat,—all their beauties offered up and promised one more time. The music had begun. There were five musicians. All the candles were burning. A movement revealed itself, a cadence; they yield to it. An aigrette shines, stops shining; it shines again, as the head leans sideways. The end of a colorful plume regains its lost color as it glides over a shoulder up to where there is shadow; it's the shadow that is between the two shoulders, now diminished, now lengthened. There is also a shadow that runs along an arm, furrows into it, and then is erased. A step is taken concretely forward, it is untaken, it is retaken, while under the immobile bodies, the legs alone sway. But where to? Because now we're in motion and up till now we'd always been stopped in our tracks. So shall we go, or what? Let's go! The black man started to thrum on his two drums with all his might. Movement, one leg advances, the arm rises so that the elbow reaches the shoulder; shoulder to shoulder, elbow to elbow, the mouth moves to meet another mouth. Why not a little bit further? The violins have begun to play at full tilt; let's go! It had been forbidden, it is not anymore. An intense odor rises, to say it is not forbidden anymore, from their necks where there is a color like the inside of shells. Let's go! This fabric bothers us. It no longer serves any purpose, since it used to serve only as a hindrance. The music intensifies the rhythm. Let's go! The black man smiles with all his big beautiful white teeth. Let's go! go! go! And for as long as they can;—and all the way to the end, while a candle goes out; two large bodies, the only ones left standing, lean, very slowly lean,—another candle goes out,—lean, lean; and all those other bodies have already lain down on the rugs.

XVIII

The vast rail network, which is no longer in use, had at first gleamed white like ruts full of water under the sky reflected in it; that whiteness had gone out;—it lights up again in red. Not far from here, the goods station continued to burn quietly through the night. From time to time, a train would explode: a great column of sparks would shoot straight up, then start to wobble. Midnight, two in the morning, three in the morning; now we will not only count the days, but the hours, and another hour arrives, while the fire silently and secretly gains ground within the charcoal heaps.

There is that other fire, which comes from below and had been at work below, in the depths of the red cave, in little bursts, in little advances like a miner, without a sound. In certain places, there were sounds, in others nothing. Day barely broke, the air was so encumbered by smoke. A rooster tried again to sing; there was the commotion of birds in the trees; they came out of their hiding places only to quickly hide again. The stench was burnt rubber mixed with bituminous coal. This is the moment when the mechanic in his dark blue shirt and black straw hat would leave his house to go to work, carrying his provision basket, but first, he would go feed the rabbits, standing behind the wire fence with grass and carrots: there was no mechanic in sight. This is the moment when all the shutters would flap as if applauding the day's arrival: they did not flap this morning. Everyone is asleep, or what if there's no one left? Under an arbor is the bowling lane; the little old man who used to pick up the pins did not pick them up the last time (when was that?); a bottle that was on the table has tipped over, it was left to empty itself drop by drop, making a puddle in the gravel that is not yet dry. The little old man had fallen on his bottom. Behind the lane there is a kind of dirt barricade meant to keep the pins from going too far; the little old man had slid right against it, his hands on his thighs, his chin on his chest, his gray beard folded over. His face was hidden by his hat, he no longer budged. He no longer made the slightest movement, not with his head, nor with his hands, nor with his feet hidden beneath his body, along with a part of his legs. No more, anyway, than those two others, a bit farther on, one lying on his stomach, his arms outstretched, revealing a wound on the side of his skull that had bled; and the second still seated at the table, his forehead resting on his folded arms. In this café they must have drunk, then fought, and then nothing more, and no one's left, except those who weren't able to leave. The bar remains wide open, with doors on both ends, one of which leads into the garden, the other onto the road. Among the over-turned tables, a little cat rummages and prowls. Bacchus on his barrel, a chromolithograph advertisement for a wine merchant, hangs crooked beside a mirror framed in black and cracked gold. Only the pendulum clock has suffered no damage. It continues to strike. It strikes twice every hour from the depths of its me-chanical sepulchre where the sound is produced with effort, as we say of a wet cough. The pendulum clock strikes six o'clock; it strikes six o'clock for the second time. Then, in the silence, a small sound like the thread of a running fountain; perhaps it's coming from the cellar? Nothing more, after; nothing more at all.

Nothing more, as far as we can see, but it's true that we can't see very far. It's like looking through tinted glass. The trees resemble blocks of basalt in form and also resemble blocks of basalt in color. The grass looked as if carnival workers had pitched their tents here. The roads, the paths that set out before you no longer led anywhere, their other end suspended in the void, as when a plank juts into the air. You had to go a fairly large distance in the direction of town; it was at the forking of two roads, right next to a metal shop. After the junction and before it, so as to control the exits, it looked as if arms were being raised in prayer and in supplication. We realized that it was pieces of the viaduct and footbridges thrown into a heap. Everything in the workshops had been taken out by the laborers, and they must have lain in wait behind it. They must have been armed, they had been attacked by the cavalry. In front of the barricade lay cadavers of horses, legs in the air, stomachs already swollen like ripe gourds. Equipment, muskets, helmets were lying around everywhere. The cavalry had attacked, then something had happened to make them retreat. The event had been inscribed, all kinds of events were written, as when we use colored ink to set words and phrases on the page. Something moved behind a hedge beneath the trees of an orchard; there were several horses without masters, kept there by the grass. And something else moves; now, it's a woman (as we see finally) who leaves along the road, pushing a wicker carriage with a waxed canvas hood and a child at each end. Because they must be sick. So, as quickly as she can, and all hunched over ...

The road. Houses. Where is she going?

Houses, villas. Completely enclosed, wide open, behind walls or barriers. Behind lilac bushes and the conifers we like because they keep their foliage in winter. Like chalets, or white with a flat roof, cement or cut stone, painted or unpainted, plastered or unplastered, and too small and generally too tall, with unsteady foundations, ridiculous and with ridiculous names; all along the wide avenue, its sidewalk planted with trees whose leaves fall one by one before yellowing.

It's a false autumn, a false end of the year. The leaves fall, making a clawing and scratching sound on the dry ground. There were the falling leaves; then we started to hear singing.

Before the song, the sound of leaves lasted a moment; rapidly the song grew and, in its turn, came to the fore.

It's when we arrive in town; the road, which is still climbing upward, opens onto a square where the hay markets used to be held, with the scale house in the middle and, next to the scale house, the weigher's station;—when they came, when they still came, they would wear their cotton-wool blend trousers, their blue blouses, their felt hats, they would run to throw themselves at the heads of their horses, launched with too much force to stop them at the right moment; and behind the horses swayed, with a strong aroma, the entire square structure, the small house on wheels, without windows;—when they came, and they don't come anymore, they will never come again.

Now, it's a troop of men; one has gray suspenders with red crosses that fall from his shoulders, and he stands in the middle; he wears army pants that no longer stay up, a garrison cap pulled down over his ears.

And he stands in the middle, this morning; and all around him is the large square of the hay market with no more hay markets.

A first group advances; the arms they raise are made thicker by the smoke that hangs after.

There are sweeping gestures of arms over faces that we can't distinguish; there are bodies that lean, that fall to the side, then someone steps forward just in time to catch them.

"Hello, over there!"

Voices.

"Are you coming?"

"Where?"

"To *Bras de Fer*."

Now there are many of them.

We can't really see anymore, we don't really know anymore. Everything moves down below, sways on its base in the darkness. As when we have sawed a tree, as when the tree is about to fall. As when we pull the rope and yell: "Timber! Timber!" And we hear the trunk crack. Those rooftops, seen in groups and ranges, are in motion. They too lean, to one side, then the other, they sway in a sky that seems to have come up from below, and, having been exhaled from below, settles over the real sky. We no longer know the real one, we will never again know the real one that remains behind it, and will remain behind it, so pure, so radiant and fixed and until the end, but not for us anymore. A separation intervenes between us and the sky. We are beneath this false sky of the Earth, come from the Earth and weighing over us, but no matter, and all the better! Those who come seem to say (they arrive from all directions) No matter! And even so you miss the cobblestones under your feet and now we are missing our center, no we no longer recognize it, we no longer know what is, nor who we are: but no matter!

Arriving in groups, arriving in troops; then another street that is flat, or nearly, and connects to another street that descends.

It's near what's below, near those poor neighborhoods, that it arose, that it began, there where they always lacked air and lacked everything: so they are used to it. In a haze, something acidic, something that makes you cough, a kind of drunkenness of the air; a drunkenness that is in the air, or could it be inside of us?

We don't know, we don't know anymore, things are moving.

Those narrow side streets where everything is already in ruins, and there are houses burning, there are some that have stopped burning, there are some whose smoke is still smoldering in the smoke, but that smoke can no longer find a place for itself, it goes back down; it is brought back down, it hangs before your face, we cough inside it, we laugh inside it, we drag it with both fists, we wear it around the neck, we trip over it. No matter! And all that's left is a square; that's where they reunite. It must be rather small, but we are not forced to recognize that it is small, because it has no outline. We can no longer distinguish anything except what's right in front of us. Before you is that ring of cobblestones, they've set up tables there; they are seated at those tables or lying underneath. Some of them are still moving, some of them will never move again. They have dragged all the tables they could find outside, forming a new kind of society where all possessions are shared, including food and drink, the barrels they brought, the bottles, the provisions they pillaged,—and where there's a sharing of bodies too, because everything is shared. They were so packed together that the entire row on one of the benches leaned with the same movement, because the man who was at one of the ends had leaned. We heard revolver shots. In a corner, an accordion continues to play out of tenacity, as a stream is tenacious or machinery that's been wound up. At the table nearest to you when you arrived, they were standing in twos, boys and girls. A large detonation filled the space again, shaking it only gradually and feebly, but then the tremor reached you from below even more intensely. We staggered once more, but it suits us. It binds us even more to one another, it makes us stand more solidly together. We start to laugh. We fire our rifles, we fire our revolvers. And now, they were all singing in chorus: quick, quick, while we still can, right? Equality and community! But one of the boys had turned to one of the girls: the cobblestones shifted again, he had wrapped his arm around her waist to keep her from falling. He looked at her, he saw that she was beautiful. He spoke to her; suddenly, he said to her: "You, you're mine!"

He continued:

"I want to show them that you're mine, I will show you to them, because you're beautiful ..."

And she, she hadn't believed it at first and she was laughing as she defended herself; but he had taken her. He was stronger after all, he had taken her by the waist. We watched him rise. We watched him rise, as if trying to escape; he had climbed onto the bench, as if to create a summit, above what was below, that base;—to try one last time, to be higher than them, and her with me, because she's beautiful and she's mine;—above those bodies, above those heads,—having thus climbed onto the bench, then he climbs onto the table.

He was yelling something, he was yelling: "You see!"

He had climbed onto the table, he was still holding the girl: "And you" (because he was speaking to her now), "you will be even higher than me!" and then he raised her in the air with both arms.

And, for a brief moment, we saw her (as if in fact it were really happening, as if it were all going to be fine),—we saw her way up there, with her long hair hanging down, her head falling backwards, her shoulders loosening ...

Then: bang! A single gunshot.

The boy and the girl collapsed together. What was below rose only a little as if to collect what fell from above, and all was covered back up. Just as when the waves come, following one another, without overtaking: because all together, all at the same level, right? And equality. He didn't have the right, so, well done. They laughed. But then (and this was the second thing) the air started to shift, and we heard screams behind it. The troop of voices came alone at first from behind the air; people yelled: "We've got it!" and then: "We've got it!" The air started to crack, the cemented cinder blocks of the air came uncemented. We surmised that there was a street, we distinguished that this street was on a slope. We saw the street tumbling toward us. We saw its cobblestones slide, then come toward us, and a part of it seemed to detach. There were faces, there were arms, faces. And those from here were looking, while those from below were coming. And again: "We've got it! We've got it! We've got it!" turning it into a chant. The voices, the feet set the tempo. The voices came, the feet came; more came still. Then we saw what these others had: gold. That's what we saw they had, because they went to get it with their two hands; they filled their pockets with their two hands. And they express a great joy, born of that gold; and yet what good is it to us? Because we can have everything for nothing, nothing can be bought anymore. But it was as if they had fallen back into the past, or a former hunger had remained in them;—and so everywhere a reawakening of the past, our thoughts were jumbled; those from below coming with their false joy, and a false, destabilizing jealousy, aimed at nothing, arose among those from here:

"Give us some ... No? Alright then! You just wait ..."

They have their military rifles, they have hunting rifles, they have automatic pistols, Brownings, knives. Kitchen knives, pocket knives. Batons. When they have nothing, they have their fists, they have their nails, they have their teeth. And everything disappeared within the noise, the calls, the groans, among the overturned tables ...

The banks were completely looted. One of the three major banks, located on the square above, was burning. Monuments with columns, made of ashstone and fake marble, with gilded iron gates, like fortresses that provoked envy at the same time as they forbid it;—so, every possible protective measure, but none of them served any use.

Nor the thickness of the walls, nor the reinforced vaults, nor the tempered steel strongboxes;—those noncombustible ceilings.

They burn. Bags are emptied out the windows, securities are stolen; people walk through the square up to their knees in money.

An airplane passes overhead.

A second passes overhead, making a great racket, barely outlined in the russet sky. At full speed, going in the same direction as the other, which is to say toward the mountains, which is to say toward the (perhaps still) fresh air, the good air, food, more security.

One more. Two. Three. An entire troop. Flights.

And some of the men are immobile, because for them, it's in their head and it's within themselves that they flee: there without anyone seeing, but just as much, just as fast, crossing expanse after expanse, space after space. To those mountainous countries around here, stitching the plains. The plains to the plains all the way to the sea, the seas to the seas. Stitching the seas together and from those seas to what is on the other side; going, always going. Going and going on and on …

Because we would end up back where we were.

We were made in such a way that the more we went, the more we returned. We couldn't not return. We saw inside of us that it was round. We considered, with amazement, this something round inside of us.

We were prisoners. Because it's round. Prisoners of what is round. Of what is perishable and round.

XIX

Hello anyway! Hello, all!

Hello! again and anyway, you from here, and you from farther away,—from the lands downstream, from the lands upstream, from towns and from hinterlands. All of the lands along the Rhône are mine, even if you are only a painted canvas stretched across nothing at all, as on a theater stage, where we act and then we roll you back up.

Even if you are nothing but lies and only for a time,—precisely because of that, perhaps, and while you are here.

You are starting to lean, you are starting to loosen, like a sail when there's less wind; so I will look at you again, love you once more,—seeing you better, loving you better because I know that I won't see you again, because I am at the end of loving you.

I said hello to you, I will say hello to you again. Because you are here, because you will no longer be here, O paintings, painted things, things stretched before us with a bit of color, and with parts that are starting to peel ...

Painting of green, blue, white, gray, painting of grass, water, rock, O valley, O double ledge, sometimes widened, sometimes narrowed. Double rocky coast with water in the space between, which is before my eyes here, then I will go to look for it farther in thought, I'll continue, starting at its two ends in thought, and I'll paint it for myself within me one more time.

Hello! again, hello to the real coast! And hello to the imaginary coast, the one I still imagine, as when the potter makes his vase, having first fashioned it in his head, then gradually coaxing his conception out of the clay, making the form descend from his head along his arms all the way down through his fingers.

Because you're here, because you're mine, because I hold you before me; and once more, in your flow, I stop you, I fix you.

Oh! you, painted lands, but you will be unpainted, so I must quickly paint you again.

The boat was moving over the water, the boat will stop moving: the boat will start to move again. I make the branch of the fig tree budge in a different kind of movement. I have the sound, the word, the color. I have lines, I have surfaces; I put in place, I make stand straight, I make rise, I make happen, I make stop happening.

Things, you alone can go,—I've seen enough of you, you don't contain me anymore, I am the one who contains you, it's my turn, you are sufficiently mine.

First taught by you, now teaching you.

Oh! taught by you, and for so long, I know; since I was very young, taught by you, because you were already coming when I didn't know how to hear, I already saw you when I didn't know how to see, Rhône-lake, and you already here;—coming with your cadences day and night, teaching me my accent, teaching me about recurrences, teaching me about duration; with your cadences, the measure of your waves; three, and three, and then three and three again, that's twelve: and then, a silence, and then you leave again.

Hammer strikes, fist strikes on the table. Let's go! And you went; and, in your wake, I went.

82

You taught me the recurrence of rhythm; so now I can go on my own.

I have you, I don't need you anymore. I use you to say hello to you.

And hello! quickly again, because you are vanishing, because everything is vanishing, because nothing will last, because nothing can last, hello one last time!

Blades of fire, raindrops, boiling oil, frying pain.

With a final voice and until my final voice.

Mirror like the one in the bedroom of a beautiful girl, one day when there is light in her heart.

Mirror, pendulum. A strike. Strike. Beating, was beating, still beating, no longer beating ...

XX

We did not see his person at first, we saw nothing at first but his sack and whatever he was carrying in his sack. We couldn't tell what it was. For a long while we saw only that white column coming, gliding above the hedge; finally, the man himself was spotted.

The hedge, at a given moment, stopped bordering the path; then the man who was carrying the sack came into view.

And he stopped at that moment, because the view revealed itself for him too;—and he started to look all around from beneath his sack which he didn't set down, which he didn't remove from his back, his sack that was not heavy, despite appearances.

It was an old basket-maker with his baskets.

A steam, a smoke, a bit of wicker fog.

We saw that construction, as when it begins to get hot in the fields and steam rises from them; lower down, there was a blue blouse, gray pants, an old face.

First he held his crossed hands in front of him; he lifted the right, it fell back down with the hat, it dangled with the hat on the side of the thigh. The left raised in its turn, it went to the beard. And then the eyes, above the beard, started to laugh on their own.

It seems not to be going very well for mankind, and thus not very well for me:—no matter!

The left hand was holding the beard, the right hand the hat; the man's two feet beneath the man in complete stillness; he looked once more at the four or five roofs, the dance floor, the fat walnut trees.

There were cherry trees and plum trees; there were tables painted green beneath the plane trees. There was a lot of rich topsoil and a bit of stony dirt. Farther back was the oak tree forest; farther back still, the sky. And there was finally, in the sky, something that started to budge, as on a white ceiling, but whiter,—while one hand was still holding the hat and the other hand was holding the beard.

And still nothing was budging above the beard except the eyes, nothing budged; and then, once more, that white column was spotted on its way.

We didn't know what we were seeing. It was white, it was gleaming and simultaneously transparent. Lower down, it was black; up top, it was like rising steam. It was something very big. We didn't know what we were seeing, we would have been amazed: but was there anyone there to be amazed?

There didn't seem to be. Anyone. The old man with the sack was coming; no one worried about him anywhere. He was now very close to the inn, displaying its barn, its stables, its sheds, its dance floor, its green tables,—but no one, not even from up close, nor in the windows, nor beneath the trees;—those four or five crooked buildings under patched roofs, with letters in new tiles, inscriptions in new tiles, designs in new tiles, a fleur-de-lys in new tiles:—nothing but these walls, nothing but these roofs.

Do you hear the chickens or the pigs squeal?

Do you hear the noise when they beat the stalks in the threshing barn, when they sharpen the scythes? And he who advances, who advances still; who goes all the way under the plane trees with the low leaves, who approaches one of the tables, who places his sack on the table, who frees one of his shoulders . . .

There, once more, he looked. He turned to the north, where the mountain rises with its vineyards. He turned to the east where the woods are. He turned to the south where the Grande-Eau flows at the bottom of a ravine. Finally he turned to the west where he came from. No one on the path, no one in the ravine, no one in the fields, no one near the vineyards.

Alone once more. Alone in the end, as he began. He passed the river, he continued for a moment longer down the road where the mile markers diligently measure the distances, among the red grasshoppers which are blue when they fly; he left the road, he took the path, having been behind the hedge with his sack loaded, it seemed, with tiny bones, baby goat carcasses bleached in the sun;—he went.

He stopped. Nothing, no one left.

Oh well! We agreed even to that. Until the end, come what may. There he is sitting in the great round shadow, pierced with holes, like a sponge; the plane tree trunks look like a woman who has just taken off her dress, which embarrasses us. He shakes the tangled beard that covers all of his face, leaving space only for the eyes.

Until the end, come what may.

He started to call, just to see. Although he knows that they won't come, he strikes his fist on the table. As when we used to sit down to drink and bang on the table and the waitress would appear. He knows that she will not come; there is no more waitress. Nothing moves anymore in the house, nor around the house. There are only sparrows descending always in groups from above the branches, searching for crumbs that they don't find anymore on the table. He goes to look, he glances through the kitchen windows; it has been abandoned. No one even took the time to put away the utensils, saucepans, plates, pots, which reach all the way to the window. That's how it is. No one left. And he has a good guess why.

Well, even so! And until the end. No matter, he said yes.

"Well, yes!"

That's what he says to himself.

"It's good even when it's bad, and it's beautiful even when it's ugly ..."

That's what he says to himself too, and he says:

"It doesn't matter."

Until the end, until the very last moment, as long as you can; as long as a tiny bit of breath is granted to you, still a wisp of breath, because the word is short (and perhaps this is precisely why it is short).

They won't stop me, you see; and once more, and until the end: Yes, always: yes.

As he says again; without us hearing anything. And anyway there is that big beard which hides that his lips are moving ...

XXI

The man shouted as he raised his whip, because the beasts were tired. We heard the shout, then the crack of the whip through the oak tree forest. To find water, we have to go all the way to the lake now; we have to lead the animals there.

The crack of the whip came, and the shout; we had to make the animals go down the cliffs by the small path down the side, then make them go back up.

Through the sand and the burning gravel, between the tufts of sweet clover, among the flies turned mean, among the roots that stick out and hang from the cracks in the ground like beards, through the risk of a landslide;—the man goes with his eight animals, because there is no more water in the wells, there is no more water in the spring, there is no more water in the stream.

And: "Ho!… Ho!…"

The fat brown beast refuses to advance. The white one extends something like two pink noses coming to meet one another, one heading down, the other heading up. Its four legs tremble, in a reflection, like four stakes planted sideways. On the surface of the water, no other wrinkles than those imparted by its nostrils, making larger and larger circles. Which the animal tugs on as it drinks, the way we tug on a rope, and the water comes, and it keeps coming, and we see the water slide beneath the skin of its neck.

In that thick steam as in a laundry;—as in a laundry room

where the women are boiling clothes;—the man, finally, having hitched up his pants, has to enter the water, too, because Brown still refuses to advance.

On the shore, at the foot of the large cliff with its red-trunked pine trees already barely visible and as if half-erased from the sky.

And descend it, go back up again; then that crossing through the woods, when the shouts come, and we hear the whip crack behind the oak trees;—then the old man with the sack, who left again under his sack, turns back around.

He saw nothing, we can't see anything; there is only, all around him, the woods.

And there is only, all around him, suffering, but as the white column continues to advance, we don't see the suffering.

We are suffering in the branches, we are suffering in the ponds. We see nothing, we hear nothing,—we suffer. There is almost nothing left of the stream; all the springs have dried up. There is suffering everywhere, and death everywhere; we hear nothing. It's the tiny little lives. You would have to crouch down, but there is no one here to do so. The man still moves beneath the white column; and here things die, but we see nothing. He is the only one still moving, we hear nothing. The lives come to an end without communication between them, nor any announcement of their end. Ah! We are forced to die alone! And how alone we are at the hour of death! Each thing, each being, alone faced with nothingness. The branch sags, every branch. The leaves have changed color: turning over on their own, they bare their pale side to the sky. The finch, this morning, went as far as it could: it returned without insects. We are suffering everywhere; even what doesn't speak, what says nothing. The little ball of pink flesh in the nest, with the little round cloudy eyes, and a beak that's too big and not yet hardened, the beak opens, opens. The very tiny and the very big. Because the earth also said something then as it groaned, and turned over, like a sick man in his bed. There are things we don't hear, but there are things we do hear. We hear the earth crack and stir beneath your shoes, it stirs beneath the mountain farther away where the vineyards are. The man walks beneath his baskets, the man walks beneath the heap of his baskets, the man walks beneath his white transparent column; a reed has fallen sideways. The entire field of reeds has fallen sideways. Everything yields, everything gives in. He is the only one walking, tracking each encounter with a movement of his head, which he lowers and carries forward, detached from the wicker column. And he alone went, and continues to go. Up to in front of and over that first large crevasse along the road, and his head crossed it first, then his feet. Over one, and he crossed it. Over this one, then comes another. Two. And here comes another one. Then the entire hill stirred. It split, split again. There is too much space for so little matter. Its back moves like a lizard beneath its scales; the man is on this back; he goes over this back, he surmounts it. He can do it; he continues. And a village appeared. Behind that bump of earth, once we have arrived at the summit, when we begin to descend; a bit below you, on the edge of the lake, in the depths of the gulf, a village with a church, an old tower, flat roofs with yellow tiles ...

"Halt!"

He was obliged to stop.

Two or three men came out from behind a wall. They stood across the road.

"Halt there!"

A rooster erupts at that moment; a chicken sings to say that the egg is made; the blue clock face of the church tells the time even so.

"Where are you going?"

"I don't know."

"Then make sure it's far!"

They gesture at him. They begin again.

"Do you understand?"

And he stands still for another brief moment, beneath what he carries; then he sees that he will have to go farther, in fact, that it will not be here.

He sees that he will not be able to enter, that he is not wanted here.

No matter!

He turned around beneath his baskets, he went back up the road; his legs were no longer visible.

The top of the white column was no longer visible.

There was no more column at all.

XXII

Just like that, they form something like republics; each village is one of these republics. Each village has gone back to the olden days when they were surrounded by walls and moats. Armed men are stationed on every path. They lie in ambush behind the walls, beneath the sheds, behind the large pear tree trunks;—and all that arrives: automobiles, bicycles, people in cars, people on horses, pedestrians—all is stopped.

Two or three days prior, the farmers of the surrounding areas had come quickly, bringing their livestock, heaping up their provisions and all the furniture they could on a deck or ladder wagon, others had found them lodging. We organized ourselves. We are a republic. We are a community. We defend ourselves. Withdrawn from fields and all work in the fields or in the vineyards, they had more time than necessary. They had four sides to themselves; when they extended a hand toward one of those sides, toward the other, another, still another, and that made four,—only one remains to them. Nothing but that side, the side of the water and that floor of water, but a floor that is not solid and does not concern them: so, they will each stand guard in turn, or they will hold meetings and give speeches at the Maison d'École. This morning, Panchaud Édouard held one before leaving, because he went fishing again with his brother, but all the others stayed. He has this side of the water, which belongs to the both of them, hence the difference; and, on his way:

92

"That's how it has to be, because now you've fallen into our care and we'll have to feed all of you ..."

Panchaud's speech. Meanwhile, gunshots.

Meanwhile, also, the ring of the school bell announcing the gathering that takes place three times per day.

The amused children watch; the women, despite everything, are amused and watch too.

Men pass by who wear their army cartridge belts over their shirts, and on their heads are large straw hats with a red drawstring.

Three here; three, four over there. Gray shirts, canvas pants, red drawstrings on their straw hats, the men pass by.

These three were designated to man the post that faces the railway tracks and a large pink farm, which they call La Chapotane; it's Louis Buchet, Corthésy, and Delessert. Slightly above this post is the one on the main road.

"Hey!" Corthésy said as he arrived.

Extending his arm, he points to what is at the other end of his arm, hanging from it; he shows us this thing over there, as if he had lifted it with his fist from the earth.

It's an automobile; they've just stopped it. The people inside step out, all bundled up, with glasses, with smocks, with veils.

And Corthésy: "They won't pass!"

Down there, with his fist outstretched, he raises the road and what is on the road, and there will be no more going over this road.

We see the white of the road among the gray and under the brown, against the white: the road, the meadows, the air, and the lake behind: "It's over!" Because we have seen to it that it be over.

And Corthésy laughs again, and the other two along with him, having looked; then, they take their guns by the strap, they take their positions.

A thousand feet in front of them is that farm La Chapotane, no longer very visible because of the bad air quality, despite its pink walls, but they have good eyes. They immediately spotted the band of men that had arrived. Now, throughout the whole countryside, there are other troops of prowlers who settle in for a day or two in the houses that people have been forced to abandon. And so, little by little, it gains, war gains ground. And destruction too, because they destroy everything, setting fire to the houses, stripping the trees of their fruit, then attacking the trees themselves. That band emerged from the woods, it entered the farm.

"Stand guard, Louis!"

It's Corthésy and Delessert, and they are talking to Louis Buchet, because he is the best shooter of the three; Buchet grabbed his gun.

He got down on his right knee in the dirt behind the low wall, upon which he placed his rifle stock; he waited.

He didn't need to wait long. The five or six men who had entered were already leaving.

"Go on!"

Twelve cartridges in the magazine, a thirteenth in the cartridge chamber, just a small front to back motion ...

"Bravo, Louis! You hit the mark. Now, the big one!... Bullseye, five points ... Bravo Louis!... They have no idea what's happening, it's comical! Watch out! Louis, get the one leaning forward ... Bravo!"

And, once more: "Bravo!" while people make pleading hand motions on the road, not far from here:

"Please!"

"No!"

"Oh! Please, please ..."

But the men of the post don't want to hear it.

The automobile they had forced to turn around now lurches

laboriously on a back road that's too steep. Another stopped, it waits, it waits for what?

Because this is our home here, you won't enter.

A kind of republic. They said to themselves: "It's just for us."

These villages are like islands; there's still a bit of sky for them, they want to keep it for themselves.

They too said to themselves: "Come what may, oh well! We have to try and carry on." We are stubborn, we don't give up so easily. We can't work in the fields, okay, we'll work at home. There's plenty of labor to be done. And still everywhere around here, even so, they speak the language of tools; they make music from mallets, they forge prayers on anvils, they hit notes by tapping nails, they line up words by hammering a stake into the ground, they create an entire sentence with the rabbet plane.

"And I," said the elder Panchaud, "I, you know ... Even if you were all dead!"

That night, pushing his boat into the water again:

"Until it's my turn to die ..."

Having had a bit too much to drink perhaps, leaning his whole body back in his clinging white swimming trunks, neck bare, arms bare, feet bare, wide shoulders, long legs, narrow waist,—leaning his whole body back against the bottom of the lake which is behind him like a whitewashed wall, beneath a plane tree branch extending horizontally so far from the trunk that it seems no longer to be a part of it;—and then, lifting his arm, to his brother:

"Are we going? ... Let's find something for them to eat ..."

Because there is still this side of the water, these fields and this tilling of the water, if the other sides are closed to us ...

Here, they continue, they continue to do. They continue to go. Toward something that they don't really know, but together, all together. The women going to each other's homes, the men helping each other. There are these posts that must be established. There are also, already, unfortunately, a large number of sick people, but we take care of them. There are many dead, many dead, my God! but we will still bury them. We do everything we can, we try to defend ourselves, even if it's probably useless. A gunshot. Scrub the kitchen floor, open all the doors and all the windows.

A gunshot. Two. Night is coming; we double the guards. From the eastern side, if you look carefully, a bit higher up than here, not so close to the water, halfway between the lake and the mountain peak which is no longer visible: it's that haze, so strange!

Unless it's smoke? Hey! Do you see?

Gunshots. No more sleep. Oh well, as long as we can keep going.

They still have a bit of sky here, soon they won't have it anymore and no one will have it anymore, no matter how far we go, with that separation intervening between us and the sky, so that we can no longer know what's happening up there: and tonight, the sun was so round, but it's no longer the sun.

It was like a moon, but three or four times bigger than the moon. Like one of those enormous round sheet metal plates that we use to bake cakes.

An enormous sun, dark red, and we could look at it.

It no longer hurts our eyes. It's as if without light, as if entirely turned into heat.

Gunshots.

XXIII

In the air, on the ground and level with the ground, under the ground, on the water, under the water, over the water, sometimes death is visible, sometimes she's not, she takes on every shape; inside of you, outside; silent, making noise.

On the public squares right in the middle of big cities, far from cities; where it's full of men, where there are no men at all, here.

Among our little fields, in our good little country, we didn't believe it, we couldn't believe it, everything was so peaceful; but yes, here she is!

Here too, here as everywhere, she comes with rapid or slow steps, the way she chooses, she who comes, not as we choose it, us.

And so we said to her: "Who are you?" We repeat: "Who are you?"

We have time to interrogate her; we have too much time, even. Time to ask her the question, to ask it once more, and again; no response.

So often, and in so many cases, all the time necessary, and much more than necessary. One on one, her and you. No one but her in the great silence, the silence of the response that doesn't come, each time a bit bigger.

Beneath the sky, behind four walls. Behind four walls, in this little room; and nothing happens here but this, which is that she comes, but he is the only one to see her.

Gavillet is here, Gavillet listens: he hears only himself. What he looks at is Gavillet, who will no longer be Gavillet. He looks at Gavillet in the mirror; there is nothing left to see but him, when he looks and sees himself. There is already no more time, nor space. There is nothing but the tiny space of a bedroom and the tinier space of the self. He has been impoverished down to his essential poverty which is about five and half feet tall by two feet wide. With no other witness but that space; that space and him. He who listens to himself, he who sees himself and also her who can't be seen. He is blind and deaf to all, someone has taken up all the space. Whether he approaches and draws closer to his image, or retreats far from it, it's never anything but him. He's grown fond of himself. In turns, he is repulsed, he is attracted. He starts to hate himself, then he loves himself. He blames himself, he pities himself; he flees, he runs after himself. Way over there, back in time, an autumn returns; Gavillet sees himself again, it's only so as not to see himself anymore, to better leave himself. Little boy in those bygone days: and he makes a fire, but the fire goes out; he cooks potatoes under the ashes, they're good, but they're quickly gone; he has finished eating them. Wherever he goes, everything passes him by. No refuge anywhere, because everything keeps shifting. We had constructed within time; we see that it's the collapse of time itself that has caused everything to collapse. And, over there, a woman who laughs, sitting under the plane trees with a bottle of lemonade, black eyes and hair in her white muslin dress, dark skin, with a red silk belt and a bare neck;—the woman laughed about everything, at everything we said to her; we said something to her, we said nothing to her, she laughed; there were five musicians seated on a plank stage decorated with pine tree branches, with insignia, with paper roses: the music had begun again; he had said to her: "Shall we?..." The woman had laughed; he had given her his arm, they had gone to the dance floor; there was a trombone, a trumpet, two bugles, a clarinet; suddenly his arms were full, she was laughing, he clasped his arms;—he tries to clasp them again, his arms are empty.

That's all finished, gone, undone. He is suddenly brought back, to what? To nothing, which is to say to himself. His shoulders slump, then he sees the gray wallpaper with its bouquets of blue flowers, which reassures him for a brief moment. He tries to reason with himself. He says: "See! It's only my imagination, it's the heat, I must have a fever, I'm sick!" He opened his door, he called out. "I'm only thirty-two years old," he said, "so why?..." He left, he goes from room to room, they're empty. He returned. "But I haven't done anything wrong, have I? I've done nothing to anyone, I harmed no one, I stole from no one, I was always honest!..." He shut his door, he turned the key in the lock. There's water in the water pot, he picks it up with both hands; he drinks. "To no one!... To no one, or did I? But no! Never; I assure you, I promise you ..." Going on this way, even so. He is not heard, he was not heard. The judgment was once more written before him on the wall where he read it; he turned his back to it: he finds it written on the other wall. He closes his eyes: it's inside him. Close your eyes, open your eyes; eyes open, eyes closed: it's still there, and he's still faced with it. Gavillet faced with Gavillet, and then there will be no more Gavillet. A forehead, two eyes, a nose: and then no more forehead, no nose, nor eyes;—something that still thinks and feels behind this forehead and then, behind this forehead, nothing more that thinks or feels. We go to meet our death through fear of death. It's so incomprehensible! This is how man is built. Man, a man: this nothing that is everything, then is nothing at all anymore. This one sees that he will no longer be, and he is so afraid of no longer being that he thinks: "Better to stop being!" This is how men are built. They go to meet death through fear of death, they flee from her in the wrong direction. Believing they are fleeing death, they go looking for her; they are attracted by that very void,—as in the mountains, standing before a precipice, when the step we take to escape it brings us to it and the fear of falling is precisely what makes us fall.

Something that feels, that will stop feeling. Something that thinks, that will stop thinking.

Gavillet opens the dresser drawer; he takes out his revolver.

XXIV

And there is the lake, and in the lake, all these people. Now, there's no choice.

The water is the color of wet dirt, with white streaks gleaming like slug trails; and all those people already there won't deter the others from coming down: these others too, but there is nothing to be done; they too have no choice.

Nothing left here, though, but a ring of dead water. Having pushed aside that thickness, the air, with both hands, those arriving stick out their heads and, from behind the haze they saw, they see and that's all there is. All distance has been erased, has been abolished. A ring of dead water, a shred of shore in a half-circle, two or three willow trees, two or three tall and big unpruned plane trees, a few bushes. They enter a round body of water like a watch face, like the others, they too have no choice but to enter the water, having fled the sand whose heat climbed above their ankles, those pebbles hot as an iron. We can no longer live on land. They venture in, they must venture in, them too; they enter. They take one step, two; they aren't used to it. They are amazed to sink further still while before them, the lake bed seems to rise—an optical illusion. They slip on the mossy pebbles, they fall. They hesitate to go farther, they must. Up to their knees, up to their stomach; then the bottom half of their bodies felt extreme relief, but it's the tops of their bodies that become impossible to bear. They venture farther, they tilt their heads back; even so, there is still the visage, the face, which is in front. They plunge their head, they miss the air; the air returns, they miss the water. Because they will have to see what it is, in the end, and how far into it we are. Those who ventured too far into the open water, no one worried about them. No one, you see, worries about anyone anymore, and even if they had called for help, no one would have intervened. Two arms emerge from the water for a moment, waving like blades of grass: it's each person's business, the battle's no longer with other individuals. There are floating bodies, they are blackened. On the surface of the dirt-colored lake, it's as if there are rivers: blackened, floating on top, drifting slowly, carried off. But some of the most recent arrivals still stand under the willow trees, seeking a vestige of coolness in their bark, or, huddled under the acacias, they rub fistfuls of foliage against their skin. A little invalid was brought there, they plopped him on the sand after they hung his suspenders from the branches; we see him, his head forward between his sharp shoulders, his mouth wide open, his ribs look three-sided like plowshares. We hear crying, we hear coughs. Some come running, they enter the water fully dressed. They pick up the little invalid, they bring him into the water. They've all had no choice, have pushed in farther and farther still. They want to live, they say to themselves: "I must," entering, entering further and further;—and they are pushed from behind, but they are watched from in front. Nothing more but a tiny round space that becomes ever smaller;—a tiny round space so as not to die at first, but then to die. And they understand. Already no voice is heard anymore, because what use would voices be? There was a great silence. And from the hush, suddenly:

"Not like this!"

A woman holding a child; she kissed him all over. He cannot understand; fortunately he cannot understand. While she still could, she brought him to her, squeezed him against her. He's asleep, he's dozing off from the heat; he won't suffer; adieu! Adieu, little one! Adieu!... Going with her kisses, quickly one more time, going to his forehead, to his little nose, to his eyes. And another time, and another time... Then, brusquely, she lifts him with both hands above her head, she advances as rapidly as she can and with the biggest steps she can...

It's as if they had been waiting for her example. There's one, then another, then still another. "I'm coming, I'm coming!" The other: "Not so fast, we can't keep up." A third: "Oh well! Me too!"

And there is only the water swirling here and there—while one man has chosen to sit in the inferno of the sand and the blaze of the star, he gathers his fists and his knees toward him.

He stays there, curled up as in the belly of a woman, his fists against his cheeks, his knees against his chest. At the moment when he will cease to exist, he holds himself as when he first began to exist; he brings about his own end by taking himself back to the very beginning, to the beginning of the beginning.

XXV

Vittoz went to stand in front of the house; he put on a woman's floral hat, one of his wife's skirts. Vittoz went to stand in front of the mirror and, simultaneously, dressed as a woman and smoked his pipe. We saw his mustache taking up a lot of space beneath the large gray straw hat, whose black silk ribbons were tied beneath his unshaved chin. He raised his head again to see himself; he saw himself through the drops of sweat that hung at his eyebrows and ran down his nose, one by one; he wiped them with his hand. With the back of his hand, he wiped them and spread them, laughing aloud at this image of himself. Then he left. He was still laughing: he laughed at everything. He heard people speaking in a house; it was only in that house that people still spoke. He stopped.

"Well yes, it's your fault. If we'd kept that money at home, we would have it ..."

A woman's voice.

"What about the interest? Ten thousand francs at six percent, that makes six hundred francs per year."

A man's voice.

"Where is this interest? Have you seen it? You fool!"

Vittoz was standing beneath the window, which was a high, ground-floor window; all he had to do was stand on tiptoe.

It's an old woman; she can barely stand up straight. An old

man, her husband, has trouble rising from his chair. We hear the grating of his chest, which rises and falls in fits and starts like old blacksmith bellows. He coughs. He tries to approach anyway. He holds the table with one hand; the other he raises in the air:

"Shut up!"

He stops, he has to catch his breath.

"You don't understand ... that ... that I have the paperwork ... the receipt ... the title ... that's what matters ... And it's worth ten thousand ... ten thousand ... and six hundred ..."

Her, then:

"Well, go and get them."

Showing him the open door (then Vittoz took a step back), showing him the way through the open door.

There is a cobblestone path, there is a big thick snapdragon, all withered; that must not have tempted him.

He fell back into his seat. He didn't budge anymore. She, also, didn't budge ...

And Vittoz, who was still laughing, had no need to keep walking away. He made one of his eyes tiny beneath the wing of his hat and between the two wide black silk ribbons, turning toward you (who wasn't there) as he gestured at the window over his shoulder with his thumb.

Here is one person who feels better than he ever has. The only thing that bothers him slightly is his tongue. He has a tongue too big for his mouth; he chews it and chews it again continually in his mouth where it is everything, and it bothers him when he speaks. But it doesn't bother him when he moves. And anyway now no one is here to stop you from doing whatever you'd like on this entire large street which slopes gently down to the lake and which Vittoz was able to follow to the end. And now gradually he notices that he's entering the water: not right away. It's because of the weight it makes around each of his shoes when he lifts them: as if, with every step, something were grabbing his foot; finally, he looks. He is even more amused. The lake has come over the top of the quay wall: Vittoz wants to doff his hat to the lake, but then he realized that the hat he was wearing is not the kind that can be removed; he curtsied to it. There is water up to the middle of his legs; this makes him laugh. We see the thick white trunks and the pale green of the plane trees emerging not from the earth now, but from the lake that reaches all the way to our doors: is it worth it, or not? This water is before you, this water is behind you. It entered the little gardens; it flowed between the blackcurrant and gooseberry bushes, the thick tufts of dahlias, the tall stalks of hollyhock; it even lapped at the feet of the bench beside the door; it ventured all the way into the kitchen. This makes Vittoz laugh; Vittoz has started to dance. Vittoz sees all this water; he jumps in on one foot, lifting his skirt with his fingertips, as he has seen demoiselles do at the balls. And then, when he'd had enough of dancing, he called. He wanted someone to see; he didn't want to be the only one enjoying himself, it's understandable; we have more fun with company. He calls as best as he can, not very well. He leaned into one of those kitchens: "Hey! Are you coming? . . . Henrioud! Is that you? Are you coming? . . ." A response. He says: "Ah! It's you . . ." And then he sees that he is mistaken. It's a cow with overly full udders, suffering from thirst and hunger, mooing from somewhere behind the canvas curtain; one cow, then another, then yet another, because they're all imitating each other. Vittoz laughed; he said: "Not you!" And then he said to himself: "There's really no one left around here!" It's like one of those Sunday afternoons when there's a festival, a festival and dance, one of those annual village shooting competitions popular in these parts. He thinks that's what it is. He says to himself that he'll have to go see. He retraced his steps. He climbs back up the whole road that he's just gone down. Ah! There's someone! "Good! That's it. Let's go speak to him." He leans over. He's in front of a barn door, he leans over as much as necessary: "Can you hear me?"—(still with that cumbersome tongue)—"Can you hear me?" The man must be sleeping, but what a deep sleep! Vittoz shakes him. Only, as he shakes him, it's as if the other were coming undone: his hands, when they move forward, remain forward, the head, when it leans to the side, stays to the side. Vittoz was rather astonished. Then, examining the man, he shrugs his shoulders: "Too bad for you!" He calls again. He is in that other area of the village: no trace of water here, quite the opposite: nothing harder and drier than the ground here; his skirt dragging on the ground raises a cloud of dust behind him; he went, he called, he began to grow impatient. "For God's sake! Is this some kind of joke?" He gets angry. A cow answers again: "Not you." A dog also answers with the cry dogs make when the moon emerges from behind the woods: "Not you! Come on!" He has forgotten that he's in a skirt; he takes trouser steps. And here are several others who are lying down; he kicks them with his foot. He's not gentle with them: "Come on! Move!" These others too, sprawled out: "What a bunch of bums!" he repeats; lying in front of their homes, seated at the foot of a wall or on the bench, their heads forward; he grabs one of those heads in his two hands; he lifts it:

"I've had enough! Do you hear me? Are you coming or not?"

But then he himself was grabbed. Two hands seize him by his underfilled blouse. There are fingers around his neck. The fingers squeeze, he opens his mouth, he rolls onto the cobblestones; the other rolls over him, continuing to squeeze, squeezing, squeezing, squeezing some more,—until there is nothing left in that throat but the tiny little noise that a fountain makes as it runs dry ...

One last boat is on the lake, but its keel is in the air; it's Panchaud's boat.

They went again while they could, the two brothers, Édouard and Jules; finally, Édouard said to Jules:

"Don't you think?"

He gestured at the water around them; he shook his head, he said:

"Fishing is done for."

He took some more of that old lake water in his hand; but it's no longer the lake, now so murky and warm.

He continued:

"Jules, don't you think?"

Jules nodded his head.

And then no more men, but it happens on its own. It happens on its own, it's apart from men. It says: "We don't need them anymore."

A little persevering task continues on its own at the very end of the gas pipes where a flame advances while the pipe melts and the flame enters a cave.

The houses lean one against the other and one after the other, seemingly sleepy. The plaster of the ceilings falls, the ceiling itself falls, the bedroom's perspective is disoriented.

The large electric turbines at the edge of the Rhône continued to spin of their own accord, still making their one thousand two hundred rotations per minute: then a large beautiful pink gleam started to jump on one foot deep in the night.

As when a tree loses its leaves, a tile falls from a roof onto the tile that has already fallen …

The group of swimmers came back up around nightfall, grains of sand stuck in the soles of their feet; the group of swimmers came back up, after having once more beaten the water with their two hands, and tucked their sliver of Marseille soap into their striped trunks. They passed in front of the barn door painted red ...

A tile falls from the roof on top of the tile that has already fallen; we couldn't believe it.

The owner couldn't believe it. The owner, who had just finished his work, was trying hard to read the paper, but it wasn't for him, it was too big. We would have had to picture the sky and the stars, the equator, the poles ... The barn door, painted red, broke in two under the weight of the arch. We couldn't. But it could for us.

The nice big dog Bari is dead at the end of his leash; the nice big dog Bari, friend to everyone in the neighborhood, faithful guardian of the house, faithful guardian of the oven too, for he was the baker's dog; he guarded the oven, he guarded the house, he pulled the cart full of loaves of bread, crunchy, hot, fragrant, emitting warmth in the cool morning on the steep uphill path, so Bari would let his tongue hang out.

A bit of steam came out of his mouth that wafted from each side of his big body with its short legs.

From his nice coat with white spots and red spots, with long tufts of fur that curled at the ends.

XXVI

No relief, not in the Earth's latitude or longitude. A few tall ships, dipping well below the waterline so much were they loaded with passengers, had again sailed back up toward the Pole: they must have turned back because of the floating sheets of ice, dropped in their path in ever greater numbers. We saw that even the cardinal points themselves would not escape destruction, being limited in number, only four: one, two, three, four, we counted them quickly. Facing each of them in turn, the captain thinks: "Will you be the right one?" and he answers no. Not the north, also called septentrion, nor the south, also called Midi; and neither the east nor the west, although they each have several names. And considered one after another, listed and relisted: but not you, nor you either! The captain, leaning over the compass, sees that the direction doesn't matter. Nor the latitude, nor the longitude,— and there's no hope left to him except in that third dimension, which is height; he had to try. Neither the Earth's latitude nor longitude, but there is height, in certain places the Earth seems to sprout from the middle of itself as if to surpass itself, to escape. We have to go higher, because many had faith in them, those regions above the others—we see that they are full of folds like the folds in the robes of the saints on cathedral porches, and the swallow comes, the swallow says: "It's for me." Those rocky regions were finely sculpted with a chisel, patiently carved, and we had thought: "The rocks will provide shelter." And it's also high, it's above, it's like the ark; it's like the other great boat of God: it floats above what's submerged below;—when there was Noah, there was Noah's wife, there were pairs of every animal species. That first green level, that second gray level: many had come, and by every means, having placed their hope in those levels, having climbed to that first, climbed to that second level. They are still here, it's full of them. However, there is the torrent; the torrent speaks. That voice is heard, the voice that began a speech that won't ever end. A long night came; it was completely filled, under the hotel windows, with things said with ever more force: whispered, spoken, spoken louder, shouted;—because what was above is coming below. The snow will no longer be snow, the ice ceases to be ice; it's a modification. And things came down, but, at the same time, things climbed up. Not only the waters of the lake: here, in the torrent bed, there are continuous tremors, tiny jumps up, but all the time and without turning back. And completely white water, in its bed of rocks like fresh milk in wooden pails. We couldn't see through it, we saw only what was sticking out. A few clusters of rocks, then nothing but two or three, then nothing but two: then nothing. A bush that drooped above seemed to droop more and more, as if its branches had become heavier, and the leaves started to soak in the water. They'd had to move the watermill ...

A lone passerby advances through the forest on the carpet of needles which is as slippery as a freshly waxed parquet floor. He had seen between the branches, for a moment more, the village; he couldn't see it anymore, because the bend in the hill had come and concealed it. Then the hill became steeper again, with its pine trees, the red trunks and the dark green of their two or three feathery branches, their roots forming knots among the round pebbles pierced with holes. The walker sat down; he listened. We heard that great breathing, a bit too short as when someone has a fever. It filled all the air with its fluttering. And never any rest; so then the walker: "If it were really true!" Now it's their turn to ask themselves: Is it true? The walker throws a glance behind him, in thought; he made the houses fall. He closed his eyes to see better, he opened them again. The houses fall,—he saw a red ant carrying its egg, too big for it, make its way among the needles that were baring their tips, so that the ant had to tame them and tip them over one after another. The fire, and everywhere those ruins,—four inches of path forged by the ant. The one standing there watches: a branch reached toward him, with its leaves like a hand, and it moved amicably before him like a wave of the hand. He could hear creaking inside of his head: silence. He didn't understand a thing anymore. We are so off-kilter. So inclined, all the time, to one of our extremes or the other. Who are we? Who are we?...

And once again he closed his eyes.

He opens them again. Voices are heard. It's a group of young people, their canvas knapsacks on their backs, climbing not far from here straight ahead of them on the steep trail, and talking loudly, words in droves, all while pointing at something even higher up, in the direction they're headed ...

XXVII

Then, higher, higher still, there where the trees can't reach and the grass is the only thing that grows. Up to those seven thousand, eight thousand feet, where the people of the valley climb each summer for two months, with their herds,—because nothing can go to waste, and they know how to be satisfied with little.

They were seated, that night, in front of the chalet; there were eight of them. The day was like every other day. As usual, once their work was over, they had eaten, then they had come to rest for a moment on the long bench beside the door. They held their hands as if they didn't know what to do with them anymore, now that they no longer served any purpose. A few of them, who'd placed their hands flat on their knees, tried smoking a pipe; a few squeezed them tightly together between their thighs; a few let them hang, empty, at their sides. The eight seated there, and the coming night. Eight of them, and they don't budge. In these regions all the way up high: here, at least, won't we be left alone? It's all the way up, higher than we normally go, above mankind and the world, above the news of the world,—so that another day was able to come, which was like all the others, and won't they be safe here?

Only the great heat (here too, even here), but that happens. And, having put the animals away for the night, they let things happen as usual around them, let the darkness happen;—the darkness arrives over the feet and hands below, without a sound, as it does, while up above the light begins to turn pink, light red, dark red, light yellow, green: as when the sainfoin blooms, as when the wheat begins to ripen, as when we've just cut the grass. Us, we are already covered, because a fine ash has fallen. And there is the very first star, there are even two or three, but those that come after, that come in groups and from every side, we don't see them.

It was the time, in fact, when ordinarily they would head inside to sleep. It was precisely the moment when they would head inside. One after the other, having tapped on the bowl of their pipes to empty out the ash, they had tucked the pipes in their pockets; they had yawned. We are very high up here, we are too high; it's as if we're out of reach. They live under the same simple laws, with an easy spirit; they didn't notice anything. They didn't notice that people had come, that they were being watched. It was a group of young people, because there was no more place for them anywhere in the valley, and they had said: "Let's go up to the chalet." And with men comes war, and war came with men all the way here. Those few had thought: "They have everything you need up there, we just have to take their place." And they had come, ascending at the same time as the darkness, which spills over the last of the escarpments ahead of them before the pasture, then starts to overtake the grassy slope, which formed three big waves one on top of the other. The highest one carried the chalet on its lip. The still-spreading darkness reached it, sprawled on top of it, as when we lie flat on our stomachs, then, having stood back up, began to climb the wall of rocks. It was at that moment. The men on the bench, their pipes in their pockets, had risen. In the stable, the cows, which had been put back inside, but are never tied up, were making various noises. There were the calves whose bells had been left on; they scratched themselves with one of their hind hooves, so the bell jingled now and then. A heifer moos, the bull pants. There are also mice that drag wood around in the boiler room, where there is still a small fire in the furnace, but the men put it out before going to bed. One of the men, in fact, having taken water in his hands, scattered it over the smoldering embers; a gleam was cast against the low ceiling and the lowing ceiling beams, it vanishes; the large wooden arm that the furnace hangs from turns black as if it were charring, retreats, melts into the darkness ...

It began with a revolver shot into the air.

The men of the chalet who had not yet headed inside remained in front of the door; those who had already entered rushed back out.

No idea came to their minds; they merely saw forms approach in the darkness; they let them approach. They could have defended themselves perhaps, they could at least have locked the door, taken refuge behind it, it didn't even occur to them. Before they had recovered from their surprise, the others had yelled: "Hands in the air!" They did as they were told. The others said: "Is this all of you?" They said yes. The others said: "Well, get out of here!" Their great shock endured, they kept their hands in the air. A bright electric lamp illuminated them: we could see the men standing squeezed together, with their big beards, their blue short-sleeved canvas jackets or their shirts,—eyes wide open and with nothing inside. "Get out of here!... Do you understand?" But no, they didn't understand, and it's because they were afraid. "Leave, we're telling you!" They still didn't understand. "Go back home, we're telling you ... We're taking your place." They moved, they took a step backwards. They moved away, they moved a bit farther away, turning their heads to the side, turning them more to look back over their shoulders ...

"Faster!"

They started to run.

A gunshot rang out again. They ran, they stopped looking back.

They rolled down the first grassy hill, then the second; the rocky escarpment greeted them after. They let themselves fall down. Calling out, no longer calling out; engulfed by the night in isolation, reunited once more; separated, reassembled, lost, found;—and all the way to the gorge, to the bottom of the gorge, to the end of the gorge, where they finally stopped ...

There was a bit of light from the stars or the moon in which they stood facing each other with their hair matted to their foreheads, their shirt collars torn: they saw that they were all there. Because of the noise of the torrent, we couldn't hear their hoarse panting; when they could speak, they could barely hear the sound of their own voices. They reached their arms up toward where they had come from, they nodded their heads, they made their hands into fists. They closed their fists at the end of their arms, shrugging their shoulders. Then one of them says something, makes a plea, because, maybe, as he said, maybe indeed; and there are those stories, there are the spirits, there are those wandering souls, and they come to torment you. But the others had started to laugh. No, it's not that! It's our mistake. We didn't grasp the situation fast enough. We weren't expecting it. No signs here yet except the amount of water in the torrent bed where it moves and we see it move because of its white color;—then they say again: "It's because we didn't understand, it's because we let it happen, it's our own fault!" And another moment like this, heads down, shaking their heads; then, suddenly, they stood up straight:

"And yet here we are, even so!"

XXVIII

They came with their story, without wanting to listen to ours. They came with their anger, and the anger they felt hindered them from seeing what was happening around them. People said to them: "Give us a hand!" They said: "We don't have time." They came and went all day long, settling their own affairs: each had their own problems. Just as the village had its own. We rang the bell around noon, an announcement. We had rung the bell around noon, we rang it again in the evening. There had been landslides; the masses of fallen soil risked blocking the torrent bed: first one corvée had gone, then a second followed. And, if we had listened well, we would have already heard that big cough coming from the direction of the glaciers (which we couldn't see well, because of the first hills, but we could have heard them), but they hadn't seen anything, and they didn't hear. They had simply waited for the night to come, thinking only of setting off, as they did, once the night had come. It's them, and they climb armed with their guns carefully cleaned and oiled. Yet another pursuit of men, yet another small pursuit of men among the other great pursuits, those of the air, the water, the earth, fire. They had gone once more in the direction of the chalet. They retraced the path they had taken the night before; they retraced with the same steps the path partly skipped by them the day before, so fast had they descended. They were following an idea, it's in front of them, they could see nothing else,—they are men. When they hear the water's voice, however, and when they hear its threats, when the entire space is filled with a kind of whispering which seems to be just for them;—and, even at these heights and in the heart of the night, so close to the snow and ice, the sweat covering their bodies is bothersome. But they thought only of the plan that they had hatched together. All had been calculated and organized with great care. Since they knew the terrain in all its detail, they had been able to divide up the positions and distribute them in advance: one of them behind that slab of rock, another behind another. Once they had arrived, they only had to wait for the night to reach a bit more toward the day, as it was doing now through fewer stars. Already it was bringing its lamps inside one by one, as if it only had to extend its hand. Behind the edge of the escarpment where they stood in their turn, we saw a whiteness form on one side of the sky, as when skin forms over milk. We began to clearly distinguish objects, their contours, their forms, outlines. Oh! Once more, even so, the Earth is lifted up toward us, the Earth is offered to us: she is beautiful now, she comes forth, she presents herself to us from inside of nothing, changed by nothing, out of nothing,—and once more, and then how many times? But, for them, it was merely the signal. They had said to Firmin: "Wait for us to be in place!" He was the youngest among them and the most nimble. They went to take their places. Firmin stayed seated for another brief moment, as agreed, then stood up. A sort of large package in the form of a ball and covered with gray canvas, which we could tell was light when he grabbed it, was set next to him on the grass; the end of a rope was hanging from his belt. He reassured himself again that the others were indeed in position; then he too started off, crawling on his hands and knees. The package on his back, he headed straight for the chalet door. From rhododendron bush to rhododendron bush,

118

he advanced, advanced farther. Nothing moved. Solitude, silence; solitude everywhere and silence: this hour before the day which is not exactly the day, which is the end of sleep, but which still belongs to sleep; and in the regions below, the bird barely begins its song: here, there isn't a single bird. Only that whiteness of the sky and its reflection lingering among the grass,—through which the man advanced, crawling; then we see him stand up, he starts to run, and we see that he's barefoot.

He made no sound. Still nothing moved. Nothing moved but him. He dropped his package. He had just arrived in front of the chalet door which was only pulled shut, and in the door was a ring that corresponded to a ring in the wall. He listened again, then carefully extended an arm. He extended the other. That other arm was holding the rope; he passed it through the rings. He made one knot, he made a second; on top of the second, he made still more. Silence, tranquility; no matter where we look, nothing is visible except for the same things; grass, dirt, the heap of rocks, the heap of ice all around, and rocks;—nothing moved (except it seems that perhaps the mountain itself moves a little, but we don't believe it), no living being, no beast, no birds, deserted land, land already above and beyond life. Thus Firmin knotted the rope; after which, having retrieved his canvas ball, he skirted around the corner of the chalet. There was hay in that ball. And then, soon after a large cloud of smoke came from behind the roof, and it moved over the roof, then it leaned forward. First, it was white, it was transparent; it quickly blackened. And then, suddenly, a shout; suddenly, behind the chalet, the shout used to bring the herd in at night, to bring them out in the morning, which the beasts understand, which they obey: Ho!... and again: Ho! Ho!... Already one beast had appeared at the stable entrance, then several others appeared, pushing forward; the shout drew them outdoors, at the same time

119

as something chased them from behind, which was the smoke, as we soon found out, because it had grown even bigger, slow to rise because of the heaviness of the air, lingering, hovering ... Because there were those holes, those fissures. And the herd went rapidly outdoors, but it was not only the herd.

And: Ho! Ho! It came from among the jingling of the bells above the pasture where there were those blotches of color that spaced out as they drifted farther away:—if we had been closer, perhaps now we would have heard how hands behind the door pulled on the door and how the door was shaken, but the rope held firm.

However, those who were in their positions said to themselves: "Get ready! It's almost time." They cocked their guns. They were crouched down on their knees, their guns already aimed; they all targeted the same spot. To the left of the chalet door was a square opening just barely big enough for a head and shoulders; this was the spot. This was the target. They were just waiting for the first head to show itself. Then the action started.

Above each group of rocks, we saw a small blue ball that had been violently shot; immediately after, the head went limp in the window frame, the arms which had been thrust out began to beat against the wall.

And all the disturbed air had first pushed forward, colliding with the rock wall, it returned, it found itself faced with itself; it returned as if to meet itself in several successive waves which, clashing, ended up going in circles; and an eddy formed at their center. Gradually they calmed down: the head, over there, stopped moving, the arms in their turn went still ...

They only had to reload their rifles, Firmin only had to put more wood on the fire (it's wet wood that he places on the fire, that's why it makes so much smoke).

And it was done,—it happened at the top of the chimney, the large square chimney that rises above the hearth, all silvery with soot, the sky as its lid; there were two this time, they had climbed inside, surely helping one another, but it had been useless. One of the two bodies fell back down inside, while the other rolled along the slope of the roof, and once more the sky was like when we take a piece of laundry by two corners and shake it.

Firmin's voice was heard; he was shouting: "It's done!" And three times, four times, five times the same thing, the thick smoke continuing to rise and enter; but they'd had to, hadn't they? They had been forced into it, they had been forced to choose, with death as their only choice.

Three, four, five times, the awakened echo was lured out once more, as when we tickle the cricket in its hole: and those inside of there too, one after the other, until the last. After which the rocks split open, each giving birth to one of the men, who took a step to the side, then many steps forward. "Is it done?" They arrived. "It's done!" We saw Firmin go to meet them, waving his hat in large swoops before him. The others arrived, rifles thrown over their shoulders, not recognizing or seeing the sky. They arrived, they shouted: "It's done!" They came, they had cut the rope that had been passed through the rings of the door; they had entered, they had laughed. They had blood on their hands, they had some on their shoes. They were happy, feeling proud of themselves. Oblivious to everything, except themselves, they took these bodies, carried them outside, threw them in a heap in a corner, counting: "One, two three," counting: "That's four"; counting up to ten; and then this tenth,—then wiping their hands on the grass, ripping out tufts of it to scrub their arms, and: "So it's over, right?" Not seeing anything else, looking only at what was left for them to do. The herd had dispersed, they had to reassemble it; there were the cows to milk, there was the fire to rekindle in the hearth ...

A voice ran down the mountain again: Ho!... Ho!...

A voice went along the slopes again, climbs the slopes, goes back down: Ho! And it's the rock now that says: Ho! And three times over: Ho!

This man cracks his whip; the other, taking the other end of the pasture, also cracks his whip, and: Ho!... And now it's the chalet wall, it's the rock again, it's the sky: Ho!... Ho!... as if they wanted to help out:—then we see the beasts gradually walk toward each other, then come together like every day.

A life of the everyday. That's all; daily chores. Things found again where they had left them, and taken back, and continued, as if it would last.

And, indeed, they see nothing. They saw nothing coming, despite the announcements. 106°, 108°, 110° among the ice and snow up there, unaccustomed to it. They continue to move beneath the white sky without being surprised by it, because of the contentment they feel in their minds. From time to time they run the back of their hands over their foreheads, that's all. They shake the hanging drops of sweat from their fingers. And, from time to time, they are forced to stop, because they're out of breath: but they don't see, they don't want to see; they don't want to understand. We would understand, if we wanted to: these men, they want only to understand that they are once more the masters of their domain, and they are all the more proud because of the effort it took. They want only to understand that they are once more the masters of these things that are theirs again, they have taken them back, so pride wins out. We did it! Some started to milk, others pushed the wheelbarrow, shoveling up the manure. Noon. They tried again to eat, then sprawled in the shade. They lay on their stomachs, they pressed themselves to the ground as much as they could: but no relief came from it, already thoroughly dried up and exhausted of all lifeblood. 117°, 120° at this hour, so what's going to happen? But that's what they don't ask themselves, although we heard now and then, up there, something like explosions, as when we blow up a tree trunk, as when we packed powder into a stump that was too gnarled and deep in the ground. 120°, 124° over the glaciers, but this is our home, isn't it? they say without saying anything, because each man thinks it to himself and they all think it together: "We are here again, now we are here even more than ever, because we had to fight to take back what's ours!" And clinging with all their might to this possession, standing back up again despite everything.

The cow moos, extends its neck, sticks out its tongue; the cow lies down on its side, letting its head fall sideways and its horn sink into the mud around the pools: the cow grazes a bit, it stops grazing.

Four in the afternoon, five ...

They didn't want to believe it: they had to.

The rock wall bordering the pastures twitched as a horse twitches its skin to get rid of flies.

And on top of the wall hangs the glacier, whose lower half is like a paused waterfall: it seems the waterfall has begun to flow again.

The crevasses, still and straight, forming straight lines, bend in the middle like the arch behind the knee.

It was as if hundreds of guns were shot at the same time.

A great tornado rose to the surface with a great gust of wind, grabbing hold of the men and animals with both hands, knocking them on top of each other on their sides pell-mell, carrying off the chalet's roof.

XXIX

Everything began to go quiet; everything quieted even more, below the Earth and above, at its ends and in the space between.

Beneath each of these skies sealed on all four sides, set beside each other and separated from each other like the cells of a honeycomb; beneath each of these low vaults, in each of these caves,—where it smoked white, where it smoked gray or brown, where it smoked black.

They still thrashed about for a little while, inside,—they stopped thrashing about. They screamed, they went quiet. Everywhere in the world, on every side:—those below us, those close by, those farther away, having called, having begged, having screamed for a long time, people of every skin color;—having knelt down before their visible or invisible gods, painted, unpainted, made of stone or wood, depicted externally or internally;—having prayed to them, having cursed them; having danced, spun in circles, having played their musical instruments for them: the large tamtam, the tambours, the violin with a single string, the copper trumpets or the horn trumpets; having played the zither, having made music, prayed, danced ...

And now it's as when the little shepherd boy made a fire.

As when the little shepherd boy made a fire; he put his hands in his pockets, he left.

A gray ring, a black ring, a rust-colored ring: these large cities,

—as when the little shepherd boy makes his fire, then leaves, whistling.

No one left, anywhere. Only, perhaps, at the foot of a hedge, near where the well used to be, at the edge of the riverbeds or in what remains of a forest, between its broken columns, between its bits of columns still standing or half-leaning: then, there, bodies, when we get up close.

This body in one position, hundreds (when we look from up close); another body in another position, sprawled out and flat or folded or legs higher than the head, twisted over themselves, torn open and exposed, or still caught under the stones, with no legs, no arms, no head; many also at windows, faces glued to the wall, hands hanging a bit lower.

Hundreds, hundreds of hundreds; the majority completely still: some not entirely yet. Fingers curl, they scratch the dirt. Beneath women's hair, completely unraveled and undone, hollow backs under the napes; they roll themselves over, the front of their bodies appears. The woman is propped on her elbow, she pushes away her hair, she saw: it would have been better for her not to see. She didn't understand at first: it would have been better for her if she had never understood. And this one, farther away, hadn't moved for a long time; suddenly, he took off running; he falls on his knees, he stands back up, he falls again ...

Meanwhile, the pilot ascends.

After a long dreamless sleep, it's as if he were emerging from a kind of first death, he woke up on his cot; he recognized himself.

He touched his body. His body is intact under the intact sheet metal shed. He jumped onto his feet. He saw that his airplane had no damage either; he starts the engine.

He spots a barge on the river making its way down in the current of what's left of the water without anyone left to steer it, and at the end of the hauling ropes are the floating cadavers of horses, now pulled after having pulled. The barge landed on a sand bank. It turned sideways, it sways there, it has time. Nothing is pressing anymore. The barge leans to the side, it straightens out, it leans again, it says: "We have time." Now it's very small, because of the great height from which it is seen, it swung on its keel once more. It has time: "But do I have time?" Amidst the rumble of the engine: time, but time to do what? climbing higher; time to do what? time for what? Speeding up even so, climbing higher, climbing toward something else, because of that thick crust of fog that must be punctured; toward no kind of time at all, as if to escape time. A thousand meters, two thousand, three thousand meters;—then the man in his machine burned. The sun, back in the sky, was like a branding iron. The man in his machine kept trying to change direction through brusque turns: on every part of his body that is exposed to the sun, there is unbearable pain, as if through real contact. No matter where or how he turns, the burning is there, it comes, it binds itself to him, it enters. He is forced to go back down. Chased from above, he goes back down again, floating once more in the opacity. Naked, completely naked, the helmet, the leather clothing, and even the underclothes removed, searching through speed for the illusion of a bit of air, amidst the spurting of oil, beneath the canvases, he began the descent, he descends even more. But then, that desert, that silence arrived. The noise that he alone makes irritates and astonishes him. He seeks a response in this noise; he seeks an answer to himself from himself. He doubts that he exists, not perceiving any existence but his own anywhere. He considers himself angrily, he is a disruption. And he keeps descending, in pursuit of a resemblance and something like symmetry. He lets himself descend even more; but nothing appeared except, vaguely and through something like ash, the immense expanse of a lake. This expanse presented to him the absolute wasteland of its waters, motionless as metal, perfectly silent and fixed, bare, with no reflection, no image, no response. Closed, mute, indifferent waters that don't know, that don't see anymore, don't hear anymore.

And by the waters also repelled, and by the waters more than ever. He closes his eyes; he's made up his mind.

He lets go of the wheel. He was then like an eagle shot in flight. He arrived with all his weight; he sank, as if down a well, to the heart of the pierced water.

The water rises for a moment, all around the crash site;—it subsided; it sealed itself back up ...

XXX

After leaving the great valley, we didn't go through that other smaller valley, which opens on one side and leads to a gorge: we climbed straight toward the isolated point of the mountain, that bluff, that kind of raised edge, which looked as if someone had wanted to place something on top. But they put nothing there except for that tiny village, which lies flat and is hardly visible. There was no way to get there except by a bad trail. We climbed beneath canvas sacks, we had our canteens, we removed our jackets and collars, we rolled up our sleeves. The beginning consisted of an awful rocky embankment in full sun. At the bottom of this embankment they had built (not long ago) a large factory, where hydrocarbon was processed. We started to climb the enormous cast iron pipe, painted black, that powered the turbines, as tall as ten of you, as big around as the size of you, then went straight down the same way we climbed straight up,—and, from a distance, we had seen its line without understanding, because there are no such lines in nature.

We climbed straight up and straight ahead of us. The tiny sand, that gravel, those flat stones, never stable, were rather discouraging underfoot. Flies crashed into your face and there were those big bumblebees that can't change direction and collide with your temple, as when children shoot at you with their elder-pith pellets. The lizards were completely still, and then, in a complete shift, rapid as thoughts. We climbed. A great thirst hit us straight away, we restrained ourselves from drinking. We pressed our lips together, passing the tip of the tongue over them from time to time; we tried to regulate the rhythm of our breath, imagining that we could thus control our hearts whose beating filled our ears. And already we heard nothing but our heartbeats, and through them were isolated from the world, from the great breathing below. It was only when we stopped and after a bit of time: then the voices came back, the great voice of the waters, the river, the wind, a passing train, someone calling, a hammer tapping on a stake ...

When we climbed, and we climbed like this for about a thousand feet; there the pipe turned to the right, there too we crossed the road that leads into the gorge and continues on one side of the gorge inside strange tunnels.

We drank a bit. We lit a pipe. We sat for a moment. As we smoked our pipes we observed how it was opening already. We looked at the beautiful land. We looked at how much sun there was over the beautiful land, a thick sun through which the land appeared as in a heavily varnished painting ...

We started walking again. We continued to climb straight ahead.

Never, here, does the slope ease up, nor allow you to. It says: "It's up to you. You have to take me as I am ..." And, once more, jacket over the bag, cane across the bag, forearms crossed under the bag to diminish the weight and ease the pressure of the straps on our shoulders, straight ahead, straight up. He came from the meadows. Here, we climb as if in a balloon, only it's a balloon that doesn't climb very fast: so we have time to see. We had time to see how things really were. We saw those little meadows. They were poor, their soil was thin and bad. The people here lived on little. They lived thirty-five hundred feet higher, with even less

129

there than here, gathering things from everywhere, like foragers of everything, not harvesters of anything, finding a little bit of something in one place, another little something in another:— and so on along the entire massive slope, always on the road, and their greatest task still was being on the roads. A hard life, we saw a hard poor life written in those little meadows as we climbed: then we felt a little less sorry for ourselves. Sometimes we met a little girl in a long skirt leading a goat: a long time before reaching you, she stopped in amazement, she brought the animal to her, she pulled on the rope with all her might, because the animal, stubborn as they are, didn't want to leave the path,—but she was even more obstinate, out of fear, or respect, and how wild they are. Or there was a woman under a basket, a man under a basket, men and women still under baskets because of all they have to carry with them, their provisions, their tools, their barrels of wine, a change of clothes, not to mention a big pile of hay on the way up, a big pile of manure on the way down. And we continued on like this for another stretch of time across the meadows, then the bushes became tall, they rushed from all sides before you to meet each other. Then came the third trek, through the forest of oak and beech trees. The fine foliage, refreshing to see, of the woods below, the woods of the beginning, for we are still at the beginning.

We had to traverse these woods. We arrived, again, in the meadows. The fourth trek was across these new meadows where the villagers who live above had their first tiny village. It was like an island of meadows on the hill; from a distance, we could see the round stain, as when we have alopecia, a spot on the head where the hair has fallen out and the skin seems paler. In the middle, this village; it's a miniature village. Tiny little houses, miniature houses that still had a kitchen and a bedroom, because they would

130

come to live in them for a week or two back when there was hay and they brought the animals to graze. Usually these kinds of villages are above the real village; this one is below. We climbed beside this first little village; we wondered how it was still standing, how it hadn't already slid down the hill, perched there as when we get on our sled to speed down and we can barely hold it back with our feet. And yet it stood. And we passed by. After which, the slope became even steeper, which seemed incredible and impossible, but yes! it was true: suddenly, it drew itself up until it was completely upright, with overlapping rows of rocks and turning black because of the pine trees. Black and red, a dull red because it was under the black, and we went under the black and through that red, along the corniches as the path followed their contours. However, even here, the tree still shoots up, it soars out of the fissures, it tilts its trunk diagonally, it makes a painting with large smears over the space it hides here and there; then the immense hole reappears, we float above it. We kept climbing.

We had to climb for another long while; it was higher up than the trees. At a certain point, the slope broke. And suddenly, before you, the real village appeared, perched there above everything,—when we didn't know what to look at anymore, nor where: at the village before us or at the void behind us, because there was that great void and that great void was calling to you ...

One of these villages, which appeared brown and white from below, which would have been the color of tin from above because of its slate roofs, completely round, squeezed against itself, all squashed in there, fissured with roads, round and flat, fissured with roads,—as when children make mud pies and abandon them in the sun.

Just above was the church. There was the cemetery around the church. There was the porch protruding from one end of the church. At the other end was the large bell tower built from gray, poorly plastered stones ...

And there was no one but them on this very last day, at this very last moment.

Only them, those up there, and the bell ringer came out, the bell ringer was in front.

The bell ringer, that last morning, had just enough time left, walking all hunched over in the wind, spinning around in the wind.

A great wind started to blow; he had to hold onto the walls along the road, and then farther on hold onto the slope, searching with his foot for the ground in front of him.

When he arrived at the bell tower, he nearly barreled into the stones. Fortunately the rope was there, hanging down two or three stories, inside the bell tower, from the very top to the very bottom, through holes. He felt the rope, greasy in that spot from his use, graze his hand; he quickly closed his fist, he quickly took out his other hand.

And they, too, had a great deal of trouble. They were in their wooden bedrooms, the ceiling moved and cracked above them like a mast, the floor swayed like the deck of a ship. On this final day, they too had to grope with their hands for the door handle, grope with their feet for the threshold; they brought a foot forward with great difficulty, because the ground rose and came to meet them, or slipped away beneath them and escaped. They, too, started to spin in the wind. The wind grabbed them, the wind spun them around. Continuing anyway, risking it anyway. As things cracked here, things were moving everywhere, falling: two or three were going, then two or three farther on, in all those little streets, going up those little streets: the father, the mother, the children; the mother clutching the youngest one against her under a shawl, the others standing at her skirt, the father going first, going ahead;—as best they could, falling, standing back up, hands on their hats to stop them from flying away, closing their mouths;—all men and all women; and, one by one, they arrived ...

But now, come on down, mountains, just fall on top of them: they do not fear you anymore, they have escaped you.

Those here (and at least those), because they came; they obeyed and they came, and the bell tolled for them, and then no longer tolled.

Those here, a few of them,—though very small in appearance, all black and small in the darkness; diminished further still because they are on their knees between the pews, in their jackets made from thick, stiff fabric or skirts with many folds, leaning forward, hands together; heels, knees together and touching, folded in two over their folded knees;—as if they were already nothing and already no longer existed: but that's only in appearance.

For now the bell begins to toll again; it will toll the three times: this salutation now announces what lies ahead.

The bell tolls the first time: they saw the imperfect space open for them in front of the other space, the time that flies and flows has ceased to fly and flow for them.

The bell tolls the second time; they heard: "Are you coming?" And then, once more: "Are you coming?" The bell tolled for the third time.

And, in their new bodies, they stood up.

A Person appeared before them on the poor lace tablecloth, between the flowers of the Earth passing through, among the little lights that trembled;—suddenly, the Person was raised up, rose up. The Person started to walk and said to them: "Are you coming?" And, in their new bodies, they came forth.

The little lights stopped trembling. And, meanwhile, they arrived: they were struck from the front.

The light struck them so intensely that their eyes melted, their former eyes that knew night, and now they had eyes that no longer knew it.

Their eyes, their ears were changed; they learned to see anew, they learned to hear anew;—in that moment, they no longer dared, they stopped, they stood still: they saw that now they no longer knew how to walk.

They had to be asked again: "Are you coming?" and again: "Will you come?" And so they tried again, and they saw that they could, they saw that they had learned to walk again.

They advanced further, they started to look. They looked at length, turning to the right, to the left: they were stunned …

As if it were more, but at the same time that's all it was; as if it were what they didn't have before, but also what they already had; as if, knowing it, they knew it anew:—and at first they hesitated, and then they stopped hesitating.

They nodded their heads.

Because then, we were not deceived after all! Because then, we were not wrong to have grown attached, we were right to love despite everything!

And they said:

"Ah, this is our home!"

Translators' note

We all have an intuitive, bodily sense of what punctuation means when we're reading a text. Each punctuation choice is a stage direction from the author. We see a period, we come to a full stop. We see a comma, we pause, but not for too long, perhaps putting more emphasis on the word that follows. Maybe the comma is one in a series, and we gain momentum as we move through the sentence. If we come upon a colon, we pause with purpose, setting ourselves up for some kind of declaration or revelation. An exclamation point carries passion or urgency. A dash might lead into an explanation, a new perspective, a clarification. A semicolon tells us to halt, but that what we are about to read next is inseparable from what we read last, that these thoughts are intertwined, and yet distinct.

But what happens when an author combines two punctuation marks together in a way we're not used to seeing? How do we embody these directions? What are we being asked to do? For example, what might it mean for an author to combine a semicolon and a dash? And what if he does it over and over and over again? How does it set up the tempo of his sentences, our sense of a character's gait, of the narrator's thought patterns? What is the author asking us to see about the rhythm of his world?

Charles-Ferdinand Ramuz, one of the great Swiss writers of the twentieth century, wrote in French, but sought to capture something beyond "le bon français" in his writing. Rather than the "langue morte" of the French he learned in school, he composed a living language, something that could utter life itself. He wanted to express the texture of his native Swiss countryside, how Vaudois French is tossed around the mouth, how his countrymen walk up a mountain or down a country lane. To the horror of l'Académie Française, no doubt—but Ramuz's quest is one that is political. Leave the people their voice and their rhythm. Let them be. Let their language show us the world that they live in. In his manifesto *Raison d'être*, Ramuz proclaims: "O, accent, you are in our words, but you are not yet in our art. You are in the gestures, you are in the bearing, and even in the shuffling step of the person who returns from harvesting or pruning his vineyard: consider this gait and the fact that our sentences don't have it."

Well, thanks to Ramuz, now their art does. That Ramuz's characteristic style and play with punctuation force the reader to inhabit this Vaudois grain is manifest throughout his 1922 novel *Into the Sun*, published at the height of his career and detailing in thirty magnificently mirrored chapters how various groups and individuals in his native region react to the Earth's slow, cruel end as it tilts toward the sun and becomes far too hot for living beings. Society collapses, what used to bring us meaning vanishes, people turn on each other or finally embrace themselves, throng together in the only remaining body of water to escape the scorching sand, rob taverns of barrels of wine, ambush each other for access to higher ground, delude themselves into keeping up with routine, think only of money or only of God, succumb to the ultimate power of nature over mankind and say goodbye sweetly to the landscapes they loved.

Into the Sun is an ode to the end, and in that sense, an ode to a beginning. As a symmetrical book, it circles back to its beginning in the hope of restoring our sight, of giving us new eyes. The way it restores sight is, of course, through language, our cinematic author's lens. To travel into the sun, we must absorb Ramuz's words, let them crack us open, just as they open the environment around us, revealing the interconnectedness of all things.

The narrator of *Into the Sun* says to his beloved Rhône River, "Oh! taught by you, and for so long, I know; since I was very young, taught by you, because you were already coming when I didn't know how to hear, I already saw you when I didn't know how to see, Rhône-lake, and you already here;—coming with your cadences day and night, teaching me my accent, teaching me about recurrences, teaching me about duration; with your cadences, the measure of your waves; three, and three, and then three and three again, that's twelve: and then, a silence, and then you leave again" (p. 82). The narrator does not merely describe the cadences he has learned from his environment, he enacts them. Similarly, we see how the narrator describes the paradoxical way people attempt to escape mortality: "This is how men are built. They go to meet death through fear of death, they flee from her in the wrong direction. Believing they are fleeing death, they go looking for her; they are attracted by that very void,— as in the mountains, standing before a precipice, when the step we take to escape it brings us to it and the fear of falling is precisely what makes us fall" (p. 100). That comma followed by a dash, that slip followed by a fall.

And so how do you translate this kind of language? There is a popular adage that one does not translate the punctuation, but rather punctuates the translation. Well, dear reader, Ramuz would say that that is utter bullshit. And so do we. As Ramuz put it in a 1929 letter to Bernard Grasset, "I remember saying to myself timidly: maybe we could try to stop translating. The man who expresses himself truly does not translate. He lets the movement play out through him, letting this same movement group the words according to its will." And that is what we have also tried to do:

Let Ramuz's words speak their own movement, not according to our language, or our rules, but according to their own.

Ramuz's quest to communicate how life is truly lived went beyond punctuation and rhythm to include abrupt shifts in tense to show that everything is always happening simultaneously, that nothing is separate from anything else, that there is no such thing as a tidy chronology when we are talking about the substance of life. The havoc of nature is happening, and already happened. You are frightened because it is happening, and because you can do nothing to prevent it since it has already happened: "The avalanche descends, the great blocks tumble down like a flock of sheep. As the avalanche descends, the bang comes; the bang came toward us" (p. 20). The present tense's constant opposition to the past reveals the narrator/Ramuz still further, and his metafictional qualities are clear in this passage about the aforementioned ambush: "They only had to reload their rifles, Firmin only had to put more wood on the fire (it's wet wood that he places on the fire, that's why it makes so much smoke)" (p. 120). With the present tense in parenthesis, the all-seeing Ramuz is commenting in real time about the past actions he's recounting. In the land of Ramuz, this present is always inextricably linked with the past, with the future.

He uses repetition to the same dizzying end, amplifying the ricochets around us until we have lost our sense of time and place, swept up in the inevitable victory of the natural world: "And hello! quickly again, because you are vanishing, because everything is vanishing, because nothing will last, because nothing can last, hello one last time! Blades of fire, raindrops, boiling oil, frying pain. With a final voice and until my final voice. Mirror like the one in the bedroom of a beautiful girl, one day when there is light in her heart. Mirror, pendulum. A strike. Strike. Beating, was beating, still beating, no longer beating ..." (p. 83).

Ramuz is also notorious for his use of the ambiguous French pronoun *on*, which can mean either an impersonal "one" or the more intimate "we" or even the more distant "they." For an author who wrote deep from the nook of his Swiss villages, *on* often represents a collective entity. A way of thinking with the masses, a new way of seeing. At times we as readers are lumped in with the group, the community. When the news that the Earth is tilting into the sun first breaks in the newspapers, the people of the town do not understand the magnitude of the situation. "On the old bench painted green, which is against the barn wall, the owner, having finished his work, begins to read: but no, he hasn't understood. It's too big, that's the thing" (p. 11). But neither have we. We, too, are ignorant, cannot grasp what is right in front of us. We, too, are lacking in imagination, Ramuz informs us: "It's not for us, it's too big. Our own world is so small. Our own world goes as far as our eyes can reach; it's our eyes that create it for us ... We would have to imagine the sky, the stars, the continents, the oceans, the equator, the two poles. Yet we can only imagine the self and what we have. This self and what we have are here" (p. 11).

At other times Ramuz switches the impact of his pronouns and we are called out directly and singularly for our pointless greed—"That's how it went. Only this consolation. Only this child, but the most beloved of the children, the most pampered, the most groomed, the one who weighed the most in your arms and against your heart,—your money" (p. 32)—or for our inner shame: "A fear has hatched inside of you; everything heightens it. It makes you hold your head differently, gives your face a different color; it is painted on your face, the fear passes from your face to the face of the person you've just met" (p. 33). The constant is that Ramuz's narrator acts like an all-seeing eye—if it's in first person, an all-seeing I—a kind of eye in the sky. A God. A sun. And then suddenly this all-seeing narrator switches from *on* to *moi* in chapter V, revealing himself, the writer, as the person who sees further than the rest. Writing is what makes the sight possible.

As the novel progresses, *on* begins to take on more than the voice of the village. By the time we begin to understand that we are all one, that we have perhaps missed the point of living, *on* starts to represent the microthings none of us ever takes into account. The tiny little lives hidden away between the trees—*on souffre*, we are suffering (p. 89). In the face of the apocalypse, *on* now represents all things, which are becoming one and the same. In our translation, we kept *on* as "we" in order to keep the panpsychism of the French: "We are suffering in the branches, we are suffering in the ponds. We see nothing, we hear nothing,—we suffer" (p. 89). In fact, this is the first time the statement *we are suffering* appears in a book that is largely about suffering. We can only arrive at this suffering once we are brothers-in-arms with all things.

There comes a moment in the book when Ramuz makes his stance clear: the world is ending because we have looked "without seeing" (p. 21). And now that we are finally seeing, we are running out of time, and so there is a gluttony to the seeing. Let us see it all before it is extinguished. So that language, sometimes, has trouble catching up to the seeing, so that sometimes we must look twice, see once more, pair the comma with the dash in order to shift our rhythm and take it all in. By the end of the book, just as the kingdom of heaven has bestowed new eyes upon the people, so too has Ramuz given us—through his apocalypse, through this great death told in living language—a new way of seeing our world.

OLIVIA BAES & EMMA RAMADAN